She'd been attracted to Colt since she was old enough to feel attraction, and apparently that hadn't changed one bit. If anything, that kiss had made it a heck of a lot worse.

Mercy, he'd gotten even better at this since they were teenagers. Not that she'd expected anything less. With those hot cowboy looks, he'd no doubt had a lot of practice. That thought was something to cool the heat down just a bit.

She definitely didn't want to be another notch on Colt's bedpost.

Yes, they'd made out before, but they'd never gone further. Elise figured it was a good idea if that remained true. And the best way for that to happen was for the kiss to stop.

He pulled back, his gaze snapping to hers, then lowering right back to her mouth. "That was a mistake."

Then, he dropped another of those scalding kisses on her mouth. He cursed some more, backed away from her. "And it's also proof of why I need to put you in someone else's protective custody."

THE DEPUTY'S REDEMPTION

USA TODAY Bestselling Author

DELORES FOSSEN

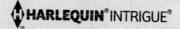

Recycling programs
for this product may
not exist in your area.

ISBN-13: 978-0-373-69818-9

The Deputy's Redemption

Copyright © 2015 by Delores Fossen

This edition published by arrangement with Harlequin Books S.A.

For questions and comments about the quality of this book, please contact us at CustomerService@Harlequin.com.

Printed in U.S.A.

Delores Fossen, a *USA TODAY* bestselling author, has sold over fifty novels with millions of copies of her books in print worldwide. She's received the Booksellers' Best Award and the RT Reviewers' Choice Award, and was a finalist for a prestigious RITA® Award. You can contact the author through her webpage at dfossen.net.

Books by Delores Fossen

HARLEQUIN INTRIGUE

Sweetwater Ranch Series

Maverick Sheriff

Cowboy Behind the Badge

Rustling Up Trouble

Kidnapping in Kendall County

The Deputy's Redemption

The Lawmen of Silver Creek Ranch Series

Grayson

Dade

Nate

Kade

Gage

Mason

Josh

Sawyer

Visit the Author Profile page at Harlequin.com for more titles

CAST OF CHARACTERS

Deputy Colt McKinnon—He must protect witness Elise Nichols from a hired gun even though Elise's testimony could tear his family apart and send his father to jail for murder.

Elise Nichols—Ten years ago, she left Colt behind for a city life that she thought she wanted. Now, she's back in Sweetwater Springs, and Colt is the only thing standing between her and a killer.

Jewell McKinnon—Colt's mother who's in jail awaiting trial for murder.

Robert Joplin—Jewell's lawyer. He would do anything to clear her name.

Buddy Jorgensen—Elise's former tenant. He's upset with her return to Sweetwater Springs and might be trying to send her running.

Meredith Darrow—A businesswoman who could be facing jail time because of a background investigation that Elise did on her.

Leo Darrow—Meredith's brother. He has a criminal record and might be helping his sister get back at Elise.

Chapter One

Deputy Colt McKinnon caught the blur of motion from the corner of his eye.

He hit the brakes, not hard, because there was likely some ice on the road, and he pulled his truck to a stop on the gravel shoulder.

There.

He saw it again.

Someone wearing light-colored clothes was darting in and out of the trees. Since it was below freezing and nearly ten at night, it wasn't a good time for someone to be jogging.

Colt took a flashlight from the glove compartment and got out, sliding his hand over the gun in his belt holster, and he tried to pick through the darkness to see what was going on. Thankfully, there was a full moon, and he got another glimpse of the person.

A woman.

She was running and not just an ordinary run, either. She was in a full sprint as if her life depended on it.

Colt hurried down the embankment toward her to see if anything or anybody was chasing her. There were coyotes in the woods, but he'd never heard of a pack going after a human. However, before he could see much of anything else, the woman ducked behind a tree.

"I have a gun!" she shouted.

Ah, hell.

He instantly recognized the voice. Elise Nichols. A voice he darn sure didn't want to hear at all, much less her yelling about having a gun.

Her house was a good five miles from here, definitely not close by enough for her to be on foot. So what in the Sam Hill was she doing running in the woods in the middle of the night?

"It's me—Colt," he said, just in case she thought he was a stranger.

"I know exactly who you are." Her voice was loud but very shaky. "And I have a gun."

"So do I," he snarled, and Colt drew it to prove his point.

Colt hadn't exactly expected a warm, friendly greeting from Elise, but he hadn't thought she was to the point of threatening to do him bodily harm.

"What the heck are you running from?" he asked.

She didn't jump to answer. The only sounds were the February wind rattling through the bare tree branches and his heartbeat pumping like pistons in his ears.

"I'm running from *you*," she finally answered.

Colt jerked back his shoulders. That sure wasn't the answer he'd been expecting. Nor did it make a lick of sense.

"I'm a deputy sheriff of Sweetwater Springs," he reminded Elise just in case she was drunk or had gone off the deep end and couldn't remember what was common knowledge around these parts.

And he reminded her also because her comment riled him.

"People generally don't feel the need to run from

me," he added with a syrupy sweetness that she would know wasn't the least bit genuine.

"They'd run if you were trying to kill them."

He tried not to let his mouth drop open, but it was close. "And you think that's what I'm trying to do to you?"

"I know you are. You ran me off the road about fifteen minutes ago."

He glanced around, didn't see another vehicle. But there was a road not too far away, and it would have been the one Elise would likely take to get to and from her place located just outside town. It was possible someone had sideswiped her and maybe she'd hit her head during the collision. That was the only explanation he could think of for a fish story like that one.

"Come out so I can see you," Colt told her, "and I'll drive you to the hospital."

She didn't answer.

Didn't move, either.

Fed up with Elise herself, her story, the butt-freezing night and this entire crazy situation, Colt huffed. "Get out here!" he ordered.

"Right. So you can kill me," she accused. "Then I can't testify at your mother's trial."

Good grief. Colt figured that subject would come up sooner or later. But he hadn't expected it to come up like this, with Elise accusing him of trying to kill her. His mother, Jewell, was the one about to stand trial for murdering her lover twenty-three years ago.

And Elise would be the key witness for the defense.

That alone was plenty bad enough because Colt figured his mom had indeed killed the guy. Anything that Elise would say in Jewell's defense could be a lie at best, and at worst it could tear his family to pieces.

Because Elise was expected to testify that not Jewell but rather Colt's father, Roy, had committed the murder.

No way would Colt or his brothers let that happen.

His father wasn't going to pay for Jewell's sins.

But there was also no way Colt would murder a witness to stop that testimony from happening. The badge he wore wasn't for decoration. He believed in the law. Believed that his mother, and Elise, would get what was coming to them.

Without his help.

"Come on out here," he repeated. "You probably got sideswiped by a drunk or something."

"A drunk driving a truck identical to yours," she countered.

That sent a bristle up his spine, and that bristly feeling went up a significant notch when Elise finally stepped out. He didn't see a gun, but from her stance, she looked as if she were challenging him to a gunfight in an Old West showdown.

"Call the county sheriff or the Texas Rangers," she insisted. "I know they won't try to kill me."

Colt huffed again and turned the flashlight on her. He prayed she didn't do something stupid and pull the trigger of the weapon that she claimed she was holding. It was a risk, but he figured Elise was only a liar and not a killer like his mother.

He moved the light over her face and then her body. She was wearing a pale blue coat and a stocking cap, but wisps of her light brown hair were flying in the wind and snapping against her face like little bullwhips.

And yeah, she had a gun.

Pointed right at him.

That didn't help his racing heartbeat. Nor did the

white-knuckle grip she had on the weapon. There were a lot of nerves showing in that grip.

"Put down the gun," Colt insisted.

"Call the county sheriff," she insisted right back.

Neither moved. Colt certainly didn't turn to make that call, but somehow he had to convince Elise to surrender her weapon. And he didn't want to have to wait the forty-five minutes or so that it would take the county sheriff to get out here.

"It's not like when we were kids, huh?" Elise said. The corner of her mouth lifted, but it wasn't a smile. "We used to play cops and robbers with toy guns. You were always the cop. I was the bad guy. Remember?"

In too perfect detail. Once, way too many years ago, Elise had been his best friend. The first girl that he'd kissed. Okay, she'd been his first love.

But he darn sure didn't feel that way about her now.

Hadn't felt that way in a long time, either. He wanted to ring her neck for trying to drag his dad into the middle of this murder trial mess.

Colt drew in a long, weary breath. "Look, can we just have a truce? Besides, you really do need to see a doctor. If you were run off the road, you could have bumped your head."

She touched her fingertips to her temple, just beneath the edge of the stocking cap, and Colt was stunned to see the dark liquid.

Blood.

That did it. He cursed and walked toward her. Colt lowered his gun to his side, just so she'd feel less threatened, but it was clear she was injured and needed help. Even if she didn't want that help from him.

Elise didn't lower her gun, however, and she backed up with each step he took. Colt kept watch to make sure her finger didn't move on the trigger. It didn't. And when he got close enough to her, he dropped the flashlight and snatched the gun from her hand.

He expected her to try to get it back. Or curse him for taking it, but she turned and ran.

Hell.

Not this.

He really didn't want to be chasing an injured woman through the woods at night, but Elise was the job now. She'd become that when she'd accused him of attempted murder and pointed the gun at him.

Colt shoved her gun in the back waist of his jeans, grabbed the flashlight and took off after her. For a woman with a bloody head and dazed mind, she ran pretty fast, and it took him several moments to catch up with her. He snagged her by the shoulder, spun her around and pinned her against a tree.

It didn't put them in the best position. They were now body to body and breathing hard. But at least she wouldn't be running anywhere.

Colt reholstered his gun so he could use the flashlight to get a look at her head. Yep, there was an angry-looking gash at least two inches long. Not a lot of blood, but she would have taken a hard lick to get that kind of injury.

"Did you hit your head when you went off the road?" he demanded.

She opened her mouth. Closed it. "I'm not sure." Her eyes were wide. Startled. But Colt couldn't tell if it was because she was still afraid of him or because of her injuries.

"The air bag deployed," she said a moment later. "The windshield broke."

So, something could have come through the glass and smacked her. "What happened then?"

Her mouth started to tremble, but she clamped her teeth over it. She also met him eye to eye, nudged him several inches away from her and hiked up her chin. No doubt trying to look a lot stronger than she felt.

Yeah, that was Elise.

"After I crashed, I heard someone get out of the truck," Elise finally answered. "The man was armed. Dressed like you."

Her gaze drifted from his Stetson to his buckskin coat. And lower. To his jeans and boots.

His *uniform* for this time of year.

"*Exactly* like you," she added.

"Plenty of people around here dress like me." Well, except for the badge. "Plenty of people drive trucks, too. In the dark most trucks look the same."

There was no indication whatsoever that she believed anything he was saying. Elise just kept staring at him as if trying to piece things together. But Colt figured that was better worked out at the hospital after a doctor had examined her.

Of course, he'd have to file a report. *Of course.* And he'd have to say that a witness in an upcoming murder trial had accused him of doing her bodily harm. He wasn't looking forward to having to explain himself, especially when he'd done nothing wrong. Still, that was part of the job, too.

"Come on." This time Colt hooked his arm around Elise's waist and got her moving. He was thankful when she didn't resist. Or collapse. Though she suddenly looked ready to do just that.

"I'll drop you off at the hospital," he explained, "and

then come back and have a look at your car. Where exactly did you go off the road?"

"Just a few yards from Miller's Creek. I crashed into the guardrail."

He knew the exact spot and winced. That creek was deep and icy this time of year. If her car had gone over, then she might have gotten a lot more than just a bloody gash on her head. She could have drowned or died from exposure, especially since there likely wouldn't have been anyone to come along and rescue her.

He leaned in to smell her breath. No scent of booze. But she did scowl and shoved her elbow against him to get him out of her face.

"I'm not drunk," she grumbled. "Or crazy. I know what happened, and I know what I saw."

Yes, and sometimes what a person saw wasn't the truth. But Colt kept that to himself. No sense getting in an argument about this particular incident.

Or the trial.

Though he was positive Elise hadn't seen what she thought she'd seen all those years ago, either.

"So, you crashed into the guardrail," he repeated while he continued to lead her to his truck. "What happened then?"

She took a deep breath. Paused. "I managed to bat down the air bag, and I got out on the passenger's side. I just started running."

Colt was about to remind her that she could have run for no reason. But he didn't get a chance to say anything.

The slash of lights stopped him.

Since the road was only twenty yards or so away, it wasn't unusual for a vehicle to come this way. But Elise obviously didn't feel the same.

"Oh, God." She turned and pulled him behind one

of the trees. Elise also reached down and turned off his flashlight.

Colt kept his attention on the truck. It was indeed the same model and color as his. And it wasn't going at a normal speed. It was inching closer as if the driver was looking for something.

Probably Elise.

And not for the killer-reasons that she believed but maybe the driver was trying to find her to make sure she was okay.

Still, Colt stayed put. Watching. Waiting. Wondering if he, too, had lost his bloomin' mind to hide behind a tree instead of just trying to have a chat with whoever was behind that steering wheel.

Next to him, Elise's breath was gusting now, and she had her hand clamped on his left arm like a vise. Every part of her was shaking.

The truck pulled just ahead of Colt's. Stopped. And the automatic window eased down. It was too dark for him to see inside, but he could just make out the silhouette of a driver. A man, from the looks of it.

The driver turned off his headlights.

That didn't help the prickly feeling down Colt's spine.

Nor did the other thing he saw.

He stepped from his truck, taking slow cautious steps while he looked at the ground.

And the man was carrying a gun.

Chapter Two

Oh, God. The man was back, and he would no doubt try to kill her again.

Elise didn't have any idea who he was, but at least she now knew that it wasn't Colt who was trying to murder her.

Not at the moment, anyway.

She'd seen the hatred in his eyes. Felt it, too, but thankfully that hadn't put him in a killing rage.

"Don't go out there," she warned him in a whisper when she felt Colt move.

Colt stopped but drew his gun. And he kept watch. Just as she did.

Elise's heart was in her throat now, every part of her geared up for fight or flight. She was hoping it was a fight that she could win, but it was hard to think straight with her head pounding like a bad toothache.

The man walked from the front of Colt's truck and down the shoulder of the road. Toward them. But he wasn't looking exactly in their direction. His gaze was firing all around him.

So, maybe he hadn't seen them, after all.

Part of her wanted to run out there and confront him, and the other part of her just wanted to see what he planned to do. She figured he wanted to finish what he had started on the Miller's Creek Bridge.

"Is that the guy who ran you off the road?" Colt asked, his voice barely making a sound.

"I'm pretty sure it is."

Elise had only gotten a glimpse of him. Or rather a glimpse of his clothes, specifically the midnight-black Stetson that looked identical to the one the Colt had worn since he was a teenager.

Maybe a coincidence.

But with everything else going on, she wasn't so sure. She had only been back in Sweetwater Springs for a month. Had barely unpacked her things at the house that'd once belonged to her grandparents. But since Elise had arrived, she'd known she wasn't exactly welcome in town.

"Had you seen him before tonight?" Colt continued, sounding very much like the lawman that he was.

"Earlier today, I saw someone watching me from the parking lot at the grocery store. I thought it was you."

He made a sound in his throat to indicate it hadn't been. "I need to bring him in for questioning. This could be just some kind of misunderstanding. I heard something about your previous tenant not being happy about having to give up the place when you moved back."

No, he hadn't been. In fact, the guy had trashed the house and left a rude message for her. "I know the tenant, and he's not the guy."

Colt stayed quiet a moment, watching the man walk closer to them. "Stay put," he told her.

And that was the only warning she got before Colt stepped out from cover. "I'm Deputy Colt McKinnon," he called out. "Who are you?"

It was hard to see much of anything with just the

watery moonlight, but the man didn't lift his gun in their direction, and he stopped, staring across the narrow clearing at Colt.

"Toby Gambil," he said, practically in a growl.

She repeated the name under her breath, trying to remember if she'd ever heard it. But she hadn't. And she didn't recognize that voice, either.

Elise wished she had her laptop handy so she could do a quick check to see what she could pull up on him. It was something she did almost daily. Her job as a corporate security analyst gave her access to all sorts of dirty little secrets.

And she had a bad feeling this guy had some.

"Any reason you're out here this time of night?" Colt pressed.

"Yeah. Some bimbo ran me off the road. I suspect she was drunk, and I came looking for her."

Elise frantically shook her head, but if Colt realized what she was doing, he gave no indication of it.

"You know this woman you claim ran you off the road?" Colt asked.

"Never saw her before in my life. I was just out here in Sweetwater Springs looking for an old army buddy. Got lost. Then, when I tried to get across the bridge not far from here, she smacked right into me with her car." He tipped his head to the front of his truck. "I want to find her because I'll need to make an insurance claim."

The man made it sound so innocent. As if it was all her fault. And it wasn't.

"You ran *me* off the road," Elise shouted out to him. Colt glanced back at her, scowled, but that didn't deter her. "You acted like you were trying to kill me."

The man took his time answering, and if he had any outward reaction to her accusation, he sure didn't show it. "Well, little lady, it seems we have a difference in opinion as to what happened."

His condescending nickname irritated her almost as much as his smug attitude.

"Just give me your name, and I'll be on my way," the man added. "I'll let the insurance company sort it all out."

"You already know my name," she snapped. "Because you were watching me at the grocery store earlier today. It's Elise Nichols."

Again, he didn't jump to respond. "Seems you're mistaken about that, too. It's my first night in town. Never been here before in my life. Maybe you're not thinking straight after the little wreck you caused."

Again, he was cocky. And that tone chilled her even more than the night air. It must have done the same to Colt, because he stepped in front of her.

"Let's drive back to the sheriff's office on Main Street," Colt ordered. And there was no mistaking the fact that it was an order given by a man with a badge. "I'll follow you. I can get your statement and call for a medic to come and check out Elise."

The moments crawled by, and Elise figured the guy would flat-out refuse. But he didn't. Gambil finally nodded, then shrugged and, as if he didn't have a care in the world, he strolled back to his truck.

"Just follow the signs to town," Colt instructed Gambil. "It'll take you straight to Main Street."

Colt got her moving again, staying just slightly ahead of her so that he was between her and Gambil. Once the man was inside his truck, Colt practically stuffed her inside his and hit the master switch to lock her door.

"Any chance what he's claiming is true?" Colt asked, taking out his phone. He didn't reholster his gun, and he didn't take his eyes off the other vehicle that was parked just a few yards ahead of them.

"No chance whatsoever," Elise insisted. "He ran into me, and when he got out, he was coming right at me with a gun."

"But he didn't shoot? And he didn't say anything to you?"

"No."

That's where her explanation ground to a sudden halt. Because he'd certainly had time to shoot her. Or at least verbally threaten her. She'd had to get out from beneath the air bag, exit on the passenger's side and then start running.

He could have put a bullet in her at any time.

So maybe this had all just been an accident. Except it hadn't felt like one.

And still didn't.

Colt started the engine and turned on the heater full blast. Until the warm air started to spill over her, Elise hadn't realized she was shivering. He also punched a button on his phone.

"Reed," he said a moment later. Reed as in Deputy Reed Caldwell from the Sweetwater Springs Sheriff's Office. "I need you to run a license plate." And Colt rattled off the number of Gambil's truck. Waited.

Looked at her.

Of course, no look from Colt was ever just a mere look.

They shared too much history for that, and those bedroom blue-gray eyes always had a way of cutting right through her. Elise tried not to let that happen now. In fact, she tried not to think of anything from their past—including the sizzling-hot attraction that'd once been between them.

No.

Best not to think of that.

Even though her body always reminded her of it whenever she was within breathing distance of him. Thankfully, over the past decade or so there had been plenty of distance between them, but she couldn't rely on that any longer. Not with them both in the same small town.

"Toby Gambil," Colt repeated. "Yeah, that's right. Anything suspicious on him, like maybe an arrest warrant?"

She couldn't hear what Reed said, but judging from the way Colt's mouth relaxed, the answer was no. Nothing suspicious. Well, nothing except for his behavior after he'd crashed into her with his truck.

"I'm on Ezell Road right now. I'll be bringing both Gambil and Elise Nichols in to take their statements about a car accident," Colt said to Reed. "Run a quick check on Gambil for me. And have a medic come to the station." He paused. "No, but Elise might need a few stitches."

She certainly hadn't forgotten about the cut on her head. It was still throbbing. But a few stitches were the least of her concerns.

Colt ended the call, put his truck into gear and flashed his headlights to let Gambil know they were about to leave. Elise held her breath, to see what the man would do, but Gambil eased out onto the road, and Colt followed right behind him.

It seemed, well, normal.

"You think I'm crazy," she mumbled. Heck, she was beginning to think that, too.

But the words had barely had time to leave her mouth

when she heard the sound that she didn't want to hear. Tires screeching on the asphalt.

Ahead of them, Gambil's truck sped away.

"Hell." Colt tossed his phone into her lap and slammed on the accelerator, too. "Call Reed. Tell him we might have a problem."

Elise didn't have time to feel even an ounce of justification that she'd been right about this situation. Ahead of them, Gambil fishtailed, his back tires skirting across the wintery road, but he quickly corrected the truck and went even faster.

Colt was right behind him.

"Let Reed know that I'm in pursuit of Gambil's vehicle," Colt said, his attention nailed to the road and the truck.

Even though her hands were shaking, Elise managed to pick through the numbers and find Reed's. The deputy answered on the first ring, and she began to relay Colt's message.

"Tell Colt to back off," Reed said before she'd even finished talking. "I believe Toby Gambil is an alias. I don't know who you're dealing with."

Elise knew. They were dealing with a man who'd tried to kill her. A man who was now trying to flee the scene. A man who'd likely given a fake name to a deputy sheriff who was questioning him.

There weren't many good reasons for a person to do that. She relayed what Reed had said to Colt.

"He could be dangerous," Reed added. "I'm on my way out there now, and I'll see about setting up a road-block."

The moment Elise pressed the end call button, Gambil slammed on his brakes. Colt cursed again, hit his brakes, too, but had to swerve into the oncoming lane to stop himself from plowing right into the back of Gambil's truck.

"Don't you dare say I told you so," Colt grumbled.

The thought hadn't crossed her mind. Right now, she was only worried about what Gambil might do next. After all, the man was armed, and Colt's and his trucks were now practically dead level with each other. Gambil could fire right into the cab and kill them both.

That's probably why Colt threw his truck into Reverse to drop back behind Gambil. But they didn't hold that position for long. Gambil hit the accelerator again, shooting forward like a bullet.

"Go after him," Elise insisted.

Yes, she was scared. Terrified, actually. But if he got away, they might never know who he really was and why he'd come after her like that.

Colt seemed to have a split-second debate with himself about what to do, but she must have convinced him, because he took off after Gambil.

"Watch for Reed," he told her.

She would. And she'd also try to watch for other cars. Elise prayed that everyone in Sweetwater Springs had stayed in tonight because with the way Gambil was driving, he could run into someone who happened to be in the wrong place at the wrong time.

There was a flash of red ahead of them. Gambil's brake lights. And he turned onto another road. But not just any road. The one that led to Miller's Creek Bridge where he'd first rammed into her.

"Why's he doing this?" she mumbled. "Why would he go back there?"

Colt only shook his head and kept following the man. However, they had only gone about a quarter of a mile when she heard the sound. As if the truck had backfired.

Almost immediately, Gambil started to swerve. And it got worse. His truck pitched to the right, heading straight for the ditch.

"Hold on," Colt said just as he put on his brakes. He had to career around Gambil, but he somehow managed to avoid another collision.

Gambil wasn't so lucky.

His truck left the road, going airborne when it vaulted over the raised shoulder, and the front end slammed into a cluster of small trees.

Elise had braced herself for something bad to happen, but she certainly hadn't expected *that*.

Colt and she sat there. Breaths sawing. Her heartbeat going like crazy. But Gambil didn't get out of the truck.

"Call Reed again," Colt told her. "Let him know where we are." And with that, he shifted his gun and opened his door.

"You're not going out there." However, she was talking to the wind because Colt was indeed going out there.

"If you move, I'll arrest you," Colt growled at her. He also shot her a warning scowl to go along with that and started toward Gambil.

Only then did Elise remember that Colt still had her gun, and she didn't like the idea of him not having some kind of backup.

Not that she would be of much help.

At best she was a lousy shot, a disgrace for someone raised on a Texas ranch, but if Gambil came out with guns blazing, she might have been able to scare him by firing over his head or something.

Now, she didn't even have that option.

With her stomach churning and her heart in her throat, she watched as Colt approached the truck. He took slow, cautious steps, his attention pinned to the driver's side.

His gun, too.

He had it pointed right at Gambil.

Gambil's headlights were still on, cutting through the silvery fog that was drifting from the nearby creek. That, along with the moon, gave her plenty of light to see Colt's expression when he threw open Gambil's door. He froze for a moment when he looked inside.

Colt's head snapped up, his gaze no longer on Gambil but on the road. And on her.

"Get down!" Colt yelled.

Elise froze, too, wondering why the heck Colt had told her that and why he was sprinting back toward her. He jumped into the truck, threw it into gear and hit the accelerator as if their lives depended on it.

A split second later, Elise realized that it did.

Because Gambil's truck exploded into a giant ball of fire.

Chapter Three

With his phone sandwiched between his shoulder and ear, Colt waited on hold while he watched the medic put some stitches on the side of Elise's head. She didn't even wince. Didn't even seem to notice.

Because her attention was nailed to Colt.

She was no doubt on the edge of her seat, waiting for answers about why this nightmare had happened, but Colt figured those answers might be a long time coming.

Especially since their suspect was dead.

Now he needed to find answers to a couple of whys. Why had Gambil come after Elise in the first place? And why had the explosives been in the truck?

Colt had only gotten a glimpse of the device on the ceiling of the truck, but he'd recognized the type of explosive and figured it was time to get out of there. He'd been lucky that he'd gotten far enough away to get only a few nicks and cuts from the flying debris. A couple of seconds later and he would have been a dead man, too.

Yeah, he definitely wanted to know why, and that started with learning everything about Gambil that there was to know.

There was a slight sound on the other end of the line to indicate he'd been taken off hold, and he heard Reed's voice. "It's not good, Colt."

Hell. Colt had already had his fill of bad news for the night and didn't want more. "I'm listening."

"We just fished Gambil's body from the rubble, and it looks as if the explosion wasn't what killed him. He already had a gunshot wound to the head."

Colt was about to say that wasn't possible, but then he remembered the sound that he'd heard right before Gambil ran off the road. A sharp pop. He'd thought it was the truck backfiring, but it could have been a gunshot.

"Check the area for any sign of a shooter," he told Reed.

Elise stood even though the medic was still trying to put a bandage on her head. Her gaze locked with his, and Colt clicked the end call button so he could fill her in on something that she wasn't going to want to hear.

"Looks like somebody shot Gambil," Colt explained.

She released her breath as if she'd been holding it. "So, all of this is real." She swallowed hard and caught onto the edge of his desk when she wobbled.

Colt went to her in case he had to stop her from falling or fainting, but the grip on the desk alone seemed to steady her enough. Still, it probably wasn't a good idea for her to be on her feet. He thanked the medic after he finished the bandage, dismissing him, and Colt took Elise by the arm and put her in the chair next to his desk.

"I know I asked you this already, but do you have any idea why Gambil wanted to hurt you?" Colt insisted.

She was shaking her head before he even finished the question. "I never saw him before today."

That didn't mean there wasn't a connection, and even though it was getting late and Elise would need to crash soon, he wanted to find out as much as he could while the events were still fresh in both their minds.

"What about your job?" Colt asked, trying for a different angle. "Are you working on anything controversial? Maybe running a background check on somebody who didn't want you to find something?"

Elise didn't immediately dismiss that. Not good. Because so far Colt hadn't been able to rule out anything. He wanted to be able to check something off his list, and he apparently wasn't going to be able to do that by eliminating anything work related.

"I'm working on two cases right now." Elise idly rubbed her head and winced when her finger raked over the freshly bandaged stitches.

"Want something for the pain?" he asked.

Elise looked at him. Maybe a little surprised by his concern.

"I just need you to have a clear head right now," he clarified. "Figured that wouldn't happen if you were in pain."

The corner of her mouth lifted for a split second, but there was no humor in it. He wasn't normally a jackass, but he also didn't feel too friendly toward someone who'd soon try to mess over his dad in a really bad way.

"Back to these two cases," Colt continued. "Did any red flags come up that could be connected to Gambil?"

"Nothing that immediately jumps to mind." She paused. "I'll have a second look, though. But this seems a little extreme for someone who might just be upset over a background check that I'm doing on them for a job."

Ah, he knew where this was going.

Right back to his family.

Colt was about to remind her that he and his brothers were all lawmen and not into witness intimidation, but there was another possible player in all of this. Best to stick to business rather than snarky comments that he really wanted to make.

"Could Gambii be connected to Buddy Jorgensen, the tenant who gave you all that trouble?" Colt asked.

She hesitated again as if surprised by the turn in the conversation. Another head shake. "I haven't heard from Buddy in nearly two weeks."

That didn't mean it wasn't connected. "He was furious about you moving back and threatened you."

And not just a threat. He'd tried to buy the place for double its value, but Elise had refused.

The rumor Colt had heard was that she planned to make the old place a small working ranch again where she could raise and train cutting horses. Ironic since Elise had been in such a big hurry to get off that ranch and out of town when she'd turned eighteen.

In a hurry to get away from him, too.

"After all of that happened, I did a background check on Buddy myself," Elise explained. "There wasn't anything that popped up that would indicate he has violent tendencies toward other people. Obviously, he didn't have quite that same level of respect for property because he spray painted graffiti on some of the walls."

Yeah, Colt had read the report that she'd filed after the incident.

Colt figured the background check on Buddy Jorgensen had been thorough since it was Elise's job. When it'd first come up that she'd be moving back to town, he'd checked on her job and learned she did investigations on potential high-level employees for several large companies. She had a solid reputation for identifying people who could be risks.

That, however, didn't mean she hadn't dropped the ball with Buddy.

And that's the reason Colt had already sent a text to Cooper, his brother, who was also the town sheriff. Cooper planned to get Buddy in for questioning first thing in the morning. In the meantime, Colt would look for some kind of connection between Buddy and Gambil.

"Have you found out anything else about the explosion?" she asked.

"Not yet. The registration for the truck leads to a dead end. No known address. But they were able to get Gambil's prints." From a couple of fingers, anyway. "Reed's already sent them to the Ranger lab, and they'll be analyzed. We might be able to get a match and find out if Toby Gambil was his real name."

Well, they would be if the prints were good enough. The explosion had done a lot of damage not just to the truck but to the man himself. Still, maybe the crime lab would be able to come up with something.

The front door flew open, bringing in a gust of the bitter-cold air and a leaf that went skittering across the floor. A man came right in with it, his pricey leather shoes crushing the leaf to bits.

Their visitor was Robert Joplin.

His mother's attorney and not someone who should be paying a visit to the sheriff's office this time of night. Judging from the scowl that he sent Colt's way, this was not going to be a pleasant conversation. Of course, pleasant and Robert Joplin had never gone together so far, and Colt figured that wasn't about to change.

"Elise," Joplin said like a concerned father. He hurried to her, plopped down his equally pricey briefcase next to her chair and caught onto her shoulders. "How badly were you hurt?"

"I'm okay, really." And she stood, easing away from him before she stepped back.

Colt didn't miss the shift in her body language. Not only had she put some distance between Joplin and her, but she also folded her arms over her chest. Like Elise, Colt had known Joplin his entire life and had no doubt seen Elise with him before, but this was the first time Colt had witnessed them together since she'd come back to testify for his mother.

Something that had pleased Joplin to the core, of course.

Before Elise and her statement, Joplin had to have known that he was defending a client who would almost certainly be found guilty. And probably still would be. However, Elise and what she'd supposedly witnessed on that day twenty-three years ago was now a game changer.

That made Elise Joplin's star witness.

But from the looks of it, an uncomfortable one.

Ditto for Joplin. His mouth tightened after she backed away from him. "I heard someone tried to kill you."

Elise lifted her shoulder. "A man tried to run me off the road, but he'd dead now."

Joplin aimed his index finger at Colt. "This is your fault. Yours and your family's. You've created a hostile atmosphere in Sweetwater Springs that's now made Elise a target."

Since things were about to turn real ugly, real fast, Colt got to his feet, but Elise stepped between them.

"I was mistaken when I called you earlier and told you that Colt was watching me," she said to Joplin. "It was this other man, Toby Gambil. He dressed like Colt and drove the same kind of truck."

So, that likely explained the weird body language

from both Joplin and her. Joplin thought he had some kind of proof of Colt's wrongdoing, and Elise was eating a little crow.

"It doesn't matter that Colt didn't do the deed himself," Joplin challenged. "He probably stirred up some of his cowboy friends to do this."

Colt moved out from behind Elise so he could face this idiot head-on. "I didn't stir up anybody. I damn sure didn't encourage anyone to kill her."

"You don't want her testifying for your mother."

"True enough. But that's only because I don't think the memories of a nine-year-old kid are reliable enough to tip the verdict of a murder trial. Especially since she didn't even tell anyone about those memories for twenty-three years."

"I didn't tell anyone what I saw because I didn't think it was important," Elise snapped, and when she swiveled toward Colt, there was some fire in her eyes. "It was only after Jewell was charged with Whitt Braddock's murder that I remembered what I saw that day."

"And what she saw was your father coming out of the Braddock cabin." Joplin punctuated that with a satisfied nod that made Colt want to smack him.

This was old news now, but it ate away at him just as it did when he'd first heard it two months ago. According to Elise, she'd been playing by the shallow creek near her grandmother's house and had seen Colt's father, Roy, leave the very cabin that all these years later would be labeled a crime scene. It'd taken that long to have all the evidence retested, the DNA identified, and the district attorney had used that to reopen what had been a missing person's case.

But now Whitt Braddock was officially dead.

Murdered.

And the only suspect had been his mother. Only her DNA and Whitt's had been found in the cabin. But Elise's eyewitness testimony could put his dad there, too.

Yeah, it ate away at him.

Because a lawyer like Joplin could maybe convince a jury that his father had just as much motive to kill Whitt Braddock as his mother did. With Elise's testimony putting his father at the scene, it might be more than enough to sway a jury and get charges filed against his father.

"I need Elise's testimony," Joplin said, stating the obvious. "I'll do whatever it takes to protect her. And more. I'll do your job, too. I've hired two private investigators to comb over every inch of the Braddock cabin and grounds again. They're looking for anything that might help with your mother's case, but the bottom line is that Elise is the best defensive weapon I have right now."

Colt wasn't disputing that, but it didn't mean he liked it, either.

Joplin huffed. "Look, I know you hate your mother because she abandoned you and your brothers—"

"She abandoned my dad, too," Colt interrupted. "Jewell walked out on her family because she couldn't bear living with the guilt of murdering her lover. But then, you've always had stars in your eyes when it comes to her, so I doubt you'll see her for the person she really is."

The anger bolted through Joplin, tightening all his muscles. "Because she's a good woman and doesn't deserve the way her so-called family has treated her."

"Enough!" Elise shouted. No stepping between them this time. She moved several feet away and glared at both of them. "Arguing about this won't help. That's what the trial is for. You can finish this debate there."

Great.

Now he had a victim scolding him like a third-grade

teacher. Of course, he shouldn't have gotten in any kind of contest with the likes of Joplin—even if everything Colt had said was true. The lawyer was crazy about Jewell, and Colt figured Joplin would do just about anything to clear her name.

Maybe even try to sway a someone's memory.

"You should go home, get some rest," Joplin said to Elise, sounding not only calmer but chastised, as well. "I can drive you there."

She motioned to Colt, or rather in his general vicinity. "I need to give a statement about what happened. That could take a while."

"Then, I can drive her home," Colt offered.

That earned him another huff from Joplin, but he didn't say a word to Colt. Instead, Joplin looked at Elise. "Call me when you're done, and no matter what time you finish, I'll come and get you."

She shrugged. Then nodded eventually. Colt was betting dollars to donuts that she wouldn't call. Nope. She was riled at both of them and would figure out her own way to get home.

Joplin picked up his briefcase and shot Colt one last warning look before he headed out.

"You actually told that jerk I was following you?" Colt asked.

That brought her gaze snapping back to his. "Because I honestly thought you were."

But the snapping and the fiery eyes didn't last. With a weary sigh leaving her mouth, she sank back down into the chair and buried her face in her hands.

Winced again, too, when she touched the stitches.

Colt didn't ask her about the pain this time, but he snatched up the phone, called the medic who'd just left and insisted that he bring some meds over for her right away. The hospital was just a few blocks up, so it wouldn't take long for him to arrive. She might need those meds just to get her statement done.

"What's going on between Joplin and you?" Colt came out and asked. "And don't say it's nothing because I detected more than a hair's worth of tension between you two."

A huff, but again no fire. "Sometimes I get the feeling that he'd like for me to say more."

Colt did a mental double take. *"More?"*

"He wants me to go through hypnosis to see if I can recall more details about Roy." Her gaze came back to his. "Like maybe blood on his clothes or looking disheveled, as if he'd just been in a fight with Whitt."

The sound that Colt made started out as a groan but got much louder. "This is a witch hunt. The only DNA found in that room was my mother's, along with a whole boatload of Whitt's blood."

"But your father was there the day Whitt went missing," she mumbled.

"So says you."

"Have you actually asked your father if he was there?" Elise challenged.

"No. I don't have to. If he'd killed Whitt, he would have owned up to it. He wouldn't have run. He darn sure wouldn't have abandoned his family."

But his father had admitted being more than just drunk that day and having some gaps in his memory. Of course, he'd just learned about his wife having an affair. And not just any ol' affair but with his sworn enemy. A man who'd been a thorn in his dad's side since they were young boys.

Colt went closer to her so she wouldn't miss a word. "If my father had killed Whitt, he would have almost certainly gotten blood on him. And when he sobered up, he would have seen it and gone to the sheriff."

He paused. "Have you actually asked Jewell about this?" Colt threw right back in her face.

The breath she took was thin and long. "Yes."

"And what did she say?" But he had to ask that through clenched teeth.

Elise made him wait several long moments before she answered. "Nothing."

Which sounded like a boatload of guilt to him. Innocent people usually spoke up to defend themselves.

Something Jewell had yet to do.

In fact, from all accounts, she wasn't even cooperating with her own attorney. Hadn't even hired him. Joplin had volunteered pro bono and had refused to back off even when Jewell had asked him to.

Because Elise and he were in the middle of an intense staring match, Colt nearly jumped out of his skin when the sound shot through the room. Elise gasped.

But it was only the phone.

Talk about losing focus.

"It's me," Reed said the moment that Colt answered. "The Rangers got an immediate hit on Gambil's prints."

That got his attention. Because that usually meant the prints were in AFIS, the national fingerprint database. "Gambil had a criminal record?"

"Oh, yeah. His real name is Simon Martinelli, and I just talked to one of our criminal informants about him." Reed paused, cursed. "Martinelli wasn't in town to scare Elise."

Mercy. There went the bristly feeling down his spine again. "Then why the devil was he here?"

"Because Martinelli's a hit man." Reed answered "He was sent here to kill Elise."

Chapter Four

"You know that I'm staying here with you tonight, right," Colt said when he pulled to a stop in front of her house.

Elise was certain that wasn't a question, and she wanted to insist that she didn't need a babysitter.

But she was afraid he'd disagree.

Because someone wanted her dead. Had even sent someone to end her life. And that someone had nearly succeeded.

She'd hoped the bone-deep exhaustion would tamp down the fear. It didn't. She was feeling both fear and fatigue, and that wasn't a good mix.

Nor was having Colt around.

However, the alternative was her being alone in her house that was miles from town or her nearest neighbor. And for just the rest of the night, she wasn't ready for the alone part. In the morning, though, she would have to do something to remedy it. Something that didn't include Colt and her under the same roof.

For now, that's exactly what was about to happen.

They got out of his truck, the sleet still spitting at them, and the air so cold that it burned her lungs with each breath she took. Elise's hands were still shaking, and when she tried to unlock the front door of her house, she dropped her keys, the metal clattering onto the weathered wood porch. Colt reached for them at the same time she did, and their heads ended up colliding.

Right on her stitches.

The pain shot through her, and even though Elise tried to choke back the groan, she didn't quite succeed.

"Sorry." Colt cursed and snatched the keys from her to unlock the door. His hands definitely weren't shaking.

"Wait here," he ordered the moment they stepped into the living room. He shut the door, gave her a stay-put warning glance and drew his gun before he started looking around.

Only then did Elise realize that someone—another hit man maybe—could already be hiding inside. Waiting to kill her.

Sweet heaven.

When was this going to end?

And better yet, why was it happening in the first place?

Elise glanced around at the living and dining rooms. The house wasn't big, so she had no trouble seeing directly into the kitchen. Colt checked it out and then headed to the back hall where there were three small bedrooms and a bath. She'd always felt so safe here. But at the moment, every shadow looked like someone lurking and ready to jump out and attack.

She held her breath, waiting, trying not to panic. The pain certainly didn't help, and even though she wanted to keep a clear head, she might have to resort to the meds that the medic had brought to her at the sheriff's office.

"Keep the curtains closed and stay away from the windows," Colt insisted. He reholstered his gun as he made his way back toward her. "You got a security system?"

She shook her head. Her grandparents would have

found it laughable that she needed such measures since there was usually no crime out here to speak of, but first thing in the morning Elise would definitely look into getting one.

"Do you have any friends from Dallas you can stay with for a while?" he asked.

Elise was about to assure him that she did, but she heard the judgmental tone in his voice. Or maybe that was her imagination working overtime, but she figured the tone was there. In Colt's mind, and likely everyone else's in town, she wasn't part of Sweetwater Springs anymore. She had chosen the city life, and while that didn't exactly make her an outcast, it didn't make her welcome, either.

"I have someplace I could stay," she answered, but then had another look around the house. No, correction.

Her home.

For two years she'd been making plans to come back here, and she'd finally gotten the chance. Not only because of Jewell's trial but because she finally had scraped together enough money to try to make the place into a working ranch again. It'd been her grandmother's dream.

Elise's, too.

And now someone was trying to snatch that away from her.

Yes, she could go running back to Dallas, to her friends and her job, but there was no guarantee that the danger wouldn't just follow her there. Maybe her best bet was to make a stand here. Of course, that might not turn out to be the safest way to go, and she'd be betting her life on it.

"You okay?" Colt walked back toward her, and he was sporting a concerned look on his face.

That's when Elise realized she was massaging the side of her head just above those stitches. She wasn't anywhere near okay, but saying it would only confirm what Colt already knew.

"Swear to me that your family didn't have anything to do with what happened tonight," she said.

Colt's eyes narrowed, clearly insulted. "I swear," he snarled. Then, he cursed. "And you'd better not accuse me of hiring that hit man to murder you."

No, she wouldn't accuse him of that. But it didn't mean the hit man hadn't been connected to Jewell's upcoming trial. The problem with that was figuring out who exactly involved with that trial would want her out of the picture.

They stood there. Gazes held. A little too close for comfort in the small living room. Of course, miles might be too close, considering how he felt about her. And how she felt about him.

Except her feelings were all over the place right now.

Elise blamed that on the pain and spent adrenaline— and the fact that Colt had saved her life—but her body wasn't going to let her forget that her childhood flame was just inches away. There'd always been an attraction between them, and she'd had that attraction verified on multiple occasions over the past decade when she'd been visiting her grandmother and had run into Colt.

Of course, the timing had always been wrong for her to act on that attraction.

He'd either been involved with someone or vice versa. Plus, there was him resenting her running off to another life. Which she had indeed done. Chasing that greener grass that hadn't turned out to be so green, after all.

Elise had always figured the attraction would just fade away. But she was rethinking that now.

Nope, it was still there. On her part, anyway.

Colt reached out, and for one heart-slamming moment, Elise thought he was reaching for her. Her stomach did a little flip-flop, and she felt something else.

That trickle of heat.

A trickle that she tried to cool down fast. But Colt cooled it for her when he didn't touch her but instead reached around her and locked the door.

"What?" he questioned, doing a double take when he looked at her face.

She saw the exact moment when it registered that it was not a question that he wanted answered aloud, and he didn't want her feeling anything for him. Didn't want to feel anything but contempt for her, either.

Elise was pretty sure they both failed at that.

It didn't mean anything would happen between them. It wouldn't. No way would Colt let something like an old attraction play into this when his father's life was essentially at stake. However, even that didn't cool the old fire that'd started to simmer again.

His mouth tightened, and he tipped his head to the sofa. "I'll need a blanket and a pillow."

"I have a guest room," she offered.

He shook his head, fast. "The sofa's fine."

Maybe because the guest room was right next to hers. Or maybe because he wanted to keep an eye on the front door in case another would-be killer showed up. That reminder didn't help with the fear or the throbbing in her head.

"It's just a precaution," Colt added, as if he'd read her mind. "Since you don't have a security system or a dog, I'd rather be out here where I can hear if anyone drives up."

She nodded, forced her feet to get moving to the linen

closet in the hall, but Elise had only made it a few steps when Colt's phone buzzed. Just like that, her heart went to her throat again, and she pulled in her breath, praying that nothing else had gone wrong.

"Reed," Colt said, answering the call.

He didn't put it on speaker, and Elise figured it wasn't a good idea for her to get close enough to him to hear what his fellow deputy was saying. However, judging from the way Colt's jaw tightened again, this wasn't good news.

"He did what?" Colt answered in response to whatever Reed had said. "No, I'll call Cooper," he added and then ended the call.

"What happened now?" she asked when Colt just stood there, glaring at the phone.

"It's Joplin. He's claiming that the attack on you is grounds for a mistrial, and he wants the charges against Jewell dismissed."

It wasn't totally unexpected news, but clearly Colt blamed her at least in part for what Jewell's lawyer was doing.

"There's more?" she asked when he just glared at her.

"Yeah, there's more." Colt pressed a button on his phone as if he'd declared war on it. "Joplin convinced the county district attorney to look into charging my father with your attempted murder."

COLT STARED AT the coffeepot, willing it to brew faster than it was. He needed another hit of caffeine now. Maybe, just maybe it'd get rid of the cobwebs before Elise finished her shower and hit him with the questions that she no doubt would have.

Questions that he still couldn't answer.

All these hours later, everything was still up in the

air. They had no leads on the identity of the person who'd hired the hit man, Simon Martinelli, and so far, Cooper hadn't managed to convince the county DA that his father was innocent.

That riled him to the core.

His dad had been through too much already what with Jewell's return to Sweetwater Springs. Now his father might not only be charged with Elise's attempted murder but also the very homicide that Colt was certain Jewell had committed.

Well, almost certain.

But even if it hadn't been her, then his father damn sure hadn't been the one to kill Whitt Braddock. That meant Colt had to figure out a way to keep his dad out of jail along with making sure Elise wasn't attacked again. It would help to find out who was behind the attempt to kill her. If he could prove his father had no part in that, then the county DA would back off.

He hoped.

Of course, there was still the problem with Elise's testimony itself. With those old memories, she could put his father at the crime scene, and because Roy had been drunk, there was no way he could refute it.

"Is that scowl for me?" Elise asked.

Colt cursed and nearly scalded his hand with the coffee he was pouring. He'd been in such deep thought about his dad that he hadn't heard her come into the kitchen. Hardly the vigilant lawman that he needed to be right now, and that seemed to be a particular problem for him anytime he was around her.

"Yes, it's for you," he mumbled.

But that lie died on his lips when he looked at her.

She was dressed simply in jeans and a red sweater, but every bit of the fear and worry was still etched on her face. Coupled with that bandage on the side of her head and the dark circles under her eyes, it was obvious that her night had been as bad as his.

Maybe worse.

After all, no one had tried to kill him in the past twelve hours.

Elise made a soft sound of frustration and stepped around him to get a cup from the cabinet. "Well, I would scowl back, but the stitches hurt when I move my face." She added a dry smile and winced to prove it.

Colt hated that attempt at bad humor, not only because he wasn't in the mood for any kind of humor but also because he knew that it had indeed hurt. Too bad the man responsible for those stitches and her pain had been blown to smithereens and couldn't give them any answers.

However, Martinelli wasn't the only way to get to the bottom of this. It would take some good old-fashioned detective work.

"I'm having inquiries made about the two people you're doing background checks on," Colt let her know, and he tipped his head to the paper on the table that he'd been using to make notes.

Obviously, she hadn't expected that because her eyes widened just a fraction. "But I didn't give you their names yet."

He gave her a flat look, tapped his badge. "Meredith Darrow and Duane Truett. I got the names from your boss when I called him in the middle of the night."

Yet something else she hadn't expected. And obviously didn't approve of. Her boss hadn't cared much for the late-night call, either, but the man had cooperated after he'd learned that Elise could have been killed.

"I knew you'd finally taken some pain meds, and I

didn't want to wake you up to get the names, so I called him. I needed to get a head start on the investigation."

That was the only apology Colt intended to issue about doing his job.

Elise walked to the table, looked over his notes and her attention stayed on the first name he'd jotted down. "'Buddy Jorgensen,'" she read off. Her former tenant. "I already told you that I ran a check on him. He doesn't have as much as a parking ticket."

"Neither do some serial killers before they're caught." Extreme, yes, but he was trying to make a point here. "It won't hurt to run another check. Is that Buddy's handiwork on the side of the barn?"

She nodded but didn't even glance out the window, though the barn was only about ten yards away and clearly visible from this side of the house. The morning sun practically spotlighted the paint that'd been splattered like blood across the gray-weathered boards. No words or drawings, just the red eyesore. Apparently, Buddy had done the same to the interior of the house, but Elise had already painted over it.

However, she couldn't paint over or dismiss the hostility that was now between Buddy and her. Buddy hadn't wanted to leave the place that he'd rented for over five years. But then he'd been more than just a tenant. He'd worked the ranch, reseeding the pasture and bringing in some livestock.

All gone now.

Buddy had taken them with him, but there were signs that Elise was planning to bring in her own cattle along with making some much-needed repairs. There was a stretch of land already marked off with stakes and small flags where she apparently intended to build a stable for the cutting horses she wanted to raise.

"I think Buddy left town, because I haven't heard from him since the paint incident," she explained. "He also apologized for the vandalism and paid for me to have it repainted."

"That's not going to get him off the suspects list," Colt insisted. "Why didn't you have the paint taken off the barn?"

"Because I'm having that one torn down. It needs a lot of repairs, and it was cheaper just to build a new one. It would be a waste of money to repaint it."

Still, it couldn't be easy to look at that every day. It wasn't a threat, but it was a reminder that someone had gotten close enough to vandalize her home and property.

Colt tapped Meredith's name. "Any reason she'd be upset with you?"

Elise paused. "No reason that she would know of yet." Another pause. "I'm not exactly giving her a favorable background check, but it'll be at least another day or two before she learns about that. I just finished my report on her yesterday. But from what I uncovered about her, she could end up facing criminal charges for misusing corporate funds."

So, that could be motive, but there hadn't been enough time for her to have hired a hit man. Well, unless Meredith had already gotten word of what would be in Elise's report. It was definitely something Colt wanted to find out.

"And what about him?" Colt asked, tapping Duane Truett's name.

"Nothing. He's squeaky clean."

Colt would still put the man under the microscope. There was a reason someone had come after Elise, and he wanted to know who and why.

"Really?" Elise said, looking at the last name on the list. "You suspect Joplin hired Martinelli?"

Colt hadn't just added it as an afterthought, he'd also underlined it. "He's got motive. If he slings enough mud at my father, or at me and my brothers, then he could get a mistrial."

And Jewell could go free.

Colt wouldn't care about that as long as going free meant Jewell left town and that there were no charges or allegations made against the rest of his family.

That wasn't likely to happen, though.

If Jewell was cleared, the blame for Whitt's murder would almost certainly fall right on his father.

"I called Joplin before I got in the shower," Elise said after she had a long sip of coffee. "I told him to back off on arresting your dad."

Colt had to replay that in his head. "And?"

She lifted her shoulder, sighed. "I don't think it did any good. Joplin's looking for a way to get the murder charges dropped against Jewell, and he thinks this is his best shot at making that happen."

"Yeah, by arresting an innocent man."

When Elise didn't argue with his *innocent* declaration, Colt glanced at her. Hard to miss her expression since they were both right in front of the coffeepot and practically elbow to elbow. He moved away from her but not before his arm brushed against her, and he felt that blasted kick.

Oh, man.

Too bad he was in between relationships right now because he would have liked to have turned this bad fire in a different direction. As it was, it went straight to Elise.

"Another scowl," she mumbled.

And he hoped she didn't ask him what this particular one was about. Best not to remind her of an attraction that he was trying hard to forget.

"Hey, I'm only testifying about what I saw," she went on. "Your father coming out of the Braddock cabin around the time that Whitt Braddock went missing. I didn't see Roy commit a murder or any other crime other than maybe trespassing. And that's what I'll say when I take the witness stand."

Colt just stared at her.

"Oh." Elise suddenly got interested in staring at her coffee. "*That.* I thought the scowl was for your father."

"It was." Not a total lie. It mostly was. "And the *that* isn't something we're going to discuss. Old water, old bridge."

It sounded good, but judging from the way Elise quickly dodged his gaze, that water and the bridge weren't quite as old as they wanted them to be.

His phone buzzed, finally, giving him a timely distraction and hopefully some good news in the process. "Cooper," he answered when he saw his brother's name pop up on the screen.

"The FBI will question Dad here in about an hour," Cooper said, skipping any greeting.

They weren't wasting any time. "I'll be there soon."

"With Elise?" Cooper immediately asked.

Colt had to think about that a moment. Best not to leave her alone until she'd worked out some other arrangement or until he'd gotten someone else to watch her. "Unless you got a better idea."

"No. Bring her. I want to talk to her."

Oh, mercy. That wouldn't be good for Elise or the investigation. And it might look as if the McKinnons were ganging up on her. Joplin would only use that to put the screws to their father.

"She's hurt and still in pain," Colt added. "She'll come with me, but I'd rather keep her out of this."

Cooper's silence was long and unnerving in a way only an older brother/boss could have managed. "Bring her," Cooper ordered and hung up.

"I heard," Elise said before Colt could fill her in. That put some steel in her cool blue eyes. "No matter what Cooper or anyone else says to me, I'm not changing my testimony."

"Good." And he meant it. "Because despite what you think of us, we're not into obstruction of justice or witness tampering."

She made a sound to indicate she didn't fully buy that. "I'll get my purse, and on the way to the sheriff's office, I can make some calls and find a safe place to go."

Colt hoped that a safe place was possible for her. Still, it wasn't his problem.

Even if it felt as if it was.

While she went back into the bedroom, he downed the rest of his coffee and reached for his coat. But reaching was as far as he got.

Something caught his eye.

Some movement out the window.

He stepped back, his gaze combing over the grounds. And he finally saw something that he definitely didn't want to see.

"What's wrong?" Elise asked the moment she came back into the room. She had obviously noticed his body language and that his attention was nailed to the barn.

"Are you expecting any workers or ranch hands today who would have a reason to go into your barn?"

"No," she answered on a rise of breath. "Why?"

"Because somebody's in there."

Colt drew his gun and headed for the front door.

Chapter Five

Elise reached for Colt to stop him from going outside, but it was already too late. He unlocked the door and hurried out onto the porch before she could tell him to wait for backup to arrive.

"Stay put," Colt insisted. "And call 911 and have Cooper get someone out here."

Just like that, her pulse revved up, and the fear returned with a vengeance. After what'd happened the night before, she figured this wasn't some coincidence.

A killer could be in her barn.

Elise made the 911 call, and the emergency dispatcher assured her that help was on the way.

The question was—would help arrive in time?

Her house wasn't exactly on the beaten path, and it would take the sheriff or one of the deputies at least twenty minutes to get out to this part of the county. That might not be nearly soon enough, and Colt was out there alone, maybe about to face down yet another person who'd been sent to murder her.

She hurried into the kitchen and took the gun from the cabinet near the fridge before she went back to the window to keep watch. She wouldn't be much backup for Colt, but maybe he'd be able to diffuse the situation before it turned violent.

Maybe.

She didn't see any movement in the barn. Didn't see Colt at first, either, but then Elise caught a glimpse of him on the side of the front porch right before he jumped down next to some shrubs. He waited, obviously listening, with his attention nailed to the gaping hole where there'd once been a barn door.

"I'm Deputy McKinnon," Colt called out, taking aim. "Come out with your hands in the air."

Elise gulped down her breath. Waited, too, and just when she thought Colt was going to have to go in after the intruder, she saw someone in the doorway of the barn. She lifted her gun. Took aim, as well. And watched as the sandy-haired man stepped out from the shadows.

Buddy.

What the heck was he doing here?

She groaned, releasing her breath and lowering her gun. But Colt certainly didn't lower his. He kept it pinned to her former tenant.

"No need for that gun," Buddy snarled, but he did keep his hands raised in the air. Even though he had a loud voice, she opened the window so she could hear him better. "I just came here to get the rest of my things."

"You're trespassing," Colt insisted.

"I'll only be here long enough to pick up a few things," he answered. Of course, that didn't explain the trespassing accusation. "After I'm finished, I'll be leaving town."

He'd told Elise that nearly two weeks ago, so either something had delayed him or he'd lied to her. She didn't like either possibility.

Buddy eased his hands down to his sides, but he didn't drop the glare that he was giving Colt. And her. Buddy snagged her gaze through the window screen, and she had no trouble seeing that he was still past the point of being angry at her.

After the night that Colt and she had had, the last thing she needed was Buddy showing up with more demands and a surly attitude. Feeling pretty surly herself, Elise shut the window and went out onto the porch so she could confront Buddy face-to-face. Obviously, though, Colt didn't like her being outside, because he shot her a split-second glare of his own.

Tough.

She stayed put.

"Got the law sleeping over here with you now?" Buddy asked her.

It wasn't just a simple question. Maybe he'd heard about the trouble from the hit man or maybe he was just trying to goad her by implying that Colt and she were having an affair.

"It's my house," she answered. "I can invite anyone I want to come here. Or sleep over. But I definitely didn't invite you."

"Didn't figure I needed an invite to get my own things," Buddy snapped.

"Well, you were wrong." Elise made sure she added her own dose of surliness to that.

Of course, it wasn't a bigger dose than Colt's.

"Go back inside," Colt warned her. Glared at her, too. "And call Cooper again to tell him I don't need backup. I can handle this on my own. But let him know that Buddy's here and that I want somebody to run a quick check on him to find out why he's still in town."

Elise debated the wisdom of him handling this alone as well as her going back inside, but Buddy didn't appear to be armed. Despite the bitter cold, he wasn't even wearing a coat, and the frayed drab gray sweatshirt hugged his beer gut enough that it didn't seem he was carrying a concealed weapon.

She made the call to Dispatch to cancel the backup and to ask for the check on Buddy, as Colt had requested, but Elise stayed put on the porch.

Oh, yes. That made Colt's glare even worse.

"You've already picked up all your things. Why'd you come back?" she asked Buddy.

He hitched his thumb toward the hayloft. "I forgot about a box of stuff still up there."

Colt glanced back at her to see if that was true, but Elise had to shrug. The ladder leading to the loft was rickety at best, and she hadn't gone up there since her return. There was no telling what was up there.

"Get the box," Colt told Buddy. "But if you remember anything else you left, call first and get permission from Elise."

That caused Buddy's nostrils to flare. "This place is my home, you know. Lived here over five years while Elise was off gallivanting in the city. If it hadn't been for me, this barn and that house would have probably fallen down by now."

"I wasn't gallivanting." Elise thought her nostrils might have flared, too. "I was working. And you were paid for any repairs you made."

She had the proof, too, since Buddy had sent her the bills, and she'd deducted the cost from his rent.

"You can't pay a person for making a house into a home," he snarled.

"And this isn't your home. It's Elise's," Colt reminded him. "It's been in her family since well before any of us were born."

"Home," Buddy repeated like profanity. His attention drifted to the place that she had staked out for a new stable. "She'll run it into the ground. She's all city now. No way can she make a go of this place."

It wasn't exactly the first time she'd faced that attitude, probably wouldn't be the last, either. But it wouldn't put her off. Especially not coming from Buddy.

"Where were you last night?" Colt demanded.

That didn't help with Buddy's angry body language, and he didn't jump to answer. "Any reason you're asking?"

"Because Elise ran into some trouble. I hope that trouble didn't come because of you."

"Not a chance. I don't want her here, but I didn't do nothing about it. If she had trouble, she probably brought it on herself."

Colt made a skeptical sound. "Or you could have helped it along. Where were you last night?" he repeated. "This time, I want an answer. If not here, then you can answer it at the sheriff's office."

"You're serious?" Buddy barked.

"Oh, yeah. Now answer me."

Buddy's glare eased up a bit, and after he did some mumbling, he scratched the scruff on his chin. "I started the night off at the Outlaw Bar, had a few drinks and left around midnight, I guess."

The incident with Martinelli had happened nearly two hours earlier, which meant Buddy wasn't involved. Well, if he was telling the truth, that is. Elise hadn't exactly trusted the man before this latest incident, and she certainly didn't trust him any more now.

"Were you with anybody at the Outlaw Bar who can confirm you were there?" Colt pressed.

Buddy shook his head. "Didn't know I'd need somebody to vouch for me."

"Well, you do."

That got Buddy cursing again. "You might be wearing a badge, Colt McKinnon, but that doesn't give you any right to talk to me like this."

Colt was no doubt about to dispute that, but Elise spoke before he could.

"Did you try to have me killed?" Elise came out and asked despite Buddy's latest round of profanity.

Colt shot her another back-off glance, which she ignored. She'd been dealing with Buddy for weeks now, and she thought she might be able to tell if he was lying. Or at least she might be able to push a button or two to get him to come clean.

"Kill you?" Buddy questioned. And his mouth twitched as if threatening to smile. "Wasn't me. But I guess you got more than just me ticked off at you, huh?"

Maybe. But Elise wondered if this was all truly connected to Buddy and his venom over her not selling him the place? She'd been so quick to pin the blame on Colt's family and the testimony that she would give for Jewell, but Buddy was certainly acting like a guilty man.

"Since it's pretty clear this isn't going to be a friendly chat, I'll get that box and leave," Buddy grumbled. "If I do any more talking to you, Deputy, I should probably have a lawyer with me so you don't try to pin any trumped-up charges on me."

With that, Buddy turned and went into the barn.

Colt huffed and moved back onto the porch with her. "I really don't want you outside with Buddy still here," he insisted.

She understood Colt's concern, but she wanted to show Buddy that she wasn't afraid of him.

Even if she was.

Either the man was mentally unstable or he had a strange attachment to her childhood home.

"If you won't go inside, at least move into the doorway," Colt pressed.

Because he was genuinely concerned about her safety. Elise was, too. So, she moved back.

"Did you see Buddy's truck anywhere?" Colt asked her.

Elise had another look around the grounds. "No." And she could see clear to the end of the road that led to her house. There weren't any motels or rental properties nearby, so that likely meant Buddy had parked on the main road itself.

Where his truck wouldn't be seen.

A man with nothing to hide wouldn't do that.

"If he'd knocked on the door and asked to get the box from the barn," she said, "I would have let him. So why all the secrecy?"

"Because maybe he wants more than just that box." Colt shot her another warning glance. "And that's another good reason for you to go inside."

Since he was right, and she was tired of arguing, Elise huffed again and stepped just inside the living room. That way, she could still see the barn and help Colt keep watch but without being right out in the open.

As Colt was.

Of course, he'd argue that it was his job to take risks like that, but Elise hated that he was essentially risking his life for her.

It didn't take long for Buddy to come back out of the barn, and he was indeed carrying a cardboard box. Thankfully, he had both hands around it, which would have made it hard for him to pull a weapon.

"Walking far with that box?" Colt asked. He went down the side steps of the porch, heading straight for

Buddy. Elise moved back into the doorway so she could hear Buddy's answer.

"Not far. Just up the road." Buddy called out. He kept walking, but he glanced over at her. "I figured I'd be in and out before Elise even got out of bed. If I'd driven up, the engine might have wakened her."

Elise wasn't buying that. Of course, maybe there was nothing sinister about this and Buddy simply hadn't wanted to run into her this morning. After the argument they'd just had, she could understand why he'd want to avoid something like that.

Still…

Colt caught up with Buddy, and he had a look in the box. Elise couldn't see what was inside it, but it didn't seem to alarm Colt any more than he already was.

"It's just papers and old magazines!" Buddy yelled. "I'm not taking anything that's not mine."

Colt stepped in front of Buddy, forcing the man to stop. "Then you won't mind if I check."

He didn't wait for permission. Colt rifled through the box while Buddy's shoulders and back got even stiffer. Colt must not have found anything because after a thorough look, he stepped aside. Buddy grumbled something that she didn't catch and continued walking up the road.

Colt kept his attention on the man, but he came back onto the porch. To stand guard, she quickly realized. Protecting her again.

"I'll make some calls," she volunteered. "And get some security arrangements started. Maybe I can even get a security system installed today."

Colt huffed. "But you're insisting on staying here." He tipped his head toward Buddy. "What if he shows up again? Or what if another hit man does?" Colt didn't wait for her to answer. "Look, I know it's uncomfortable for you having me here, so I'll call the Rangers and have them send out a protection detail."

"I'm less uncomfortable than I was," she mumbled. She no doubt should have kept that to herself. "Well, about some things, anyway."

That, too. No way should she have said that aloud to Colt because he knew exactly what she meant.

He looked over his shoulder at her, and despite the fact that they'd just had the adrenaline-spiking encounter with Buddy, she saw something else in his eyes. The reason why she shouldn't put up even a smidgen of a fight about having someone guard her.

Those McKinnon eyes—and pretty much the rest of him—were playing havoc with her body.

Colt gave Buddy another glance, no doubt to make sure the man was indeed leaving. He was. And Colt took her by the arm and moved her deeper into the living room before he shut the door. He opened his mouth, closed it and opened it again only to curse.

"Hell," he mumbled, reholstering his gun.

In the same motion, he leaned in and put his mouth on hers.

Elise wasn't sure who was more surprised by that, her or Colt. She felt the tightness of his lips. For a second, anyway. And then no more tightening. It turned into a full-fledged kiss.

One that she instantly felt.

The heat rippled through her. Mouth to toes. Warming her. Then, firing her body in a really good-bad way. It brought to the surface all those feelings that she'd been trying to pretend didn't exist.

Well, the pretense was over.

The feelings existed, all right.

She'd been attracted to Colt since she was old enough to feel attraction, and apparently that hadn't changed one bit. If anything, that kiss had made it a heck of a lot worse.

Mercy, he'd gotten even better at this since they were teenagers. Not that she'd expected anything less. With those hot cowboy looks, he'd no doubt had a lot of practice. Something that cooled the heat down just a bit.

She definitely didn't want to be another notch on Colt's bedpost.

Yes, they'd made out before, but they'd never gone further than that. Elise figured it was a good idea if that continued. And the best way for that to happen was for the kiss to stop.

He pulled back, his gaze snapping to hers. His gaze then lowering right back to her mouth.

"That was a mistake," he informed her.

Then he dropped another of those scalding kisses on her mouth. He cursed some more, backed away from her. "And that's also proof of why I need to put you in someone else's protective custody."

Elise couldn't argue with that, even if that's exactly what her body wanted her to do. However, she didn't get a chance to say anything one way or the other because Colt's phone buzzed.

"It's Reed," Colt said, glancing down at the screen. He took the call, but he also looked out the front window. So did Elise, but she could no longer see Buddy.

Despite the heat and the tension still crackling between them, Elise moved closer so she could hear what Reed was saying. And she heard, all right. Something she didn't want to hear.

"We got a problem," Reed said.

"Hell," Colt mumbled. "What's wrong now?"

"I just got the results of Buddy's background check. If he's still there, you need to bring him in now."

Chapter Six

Colt glanced through the report that Reed handed him, and he cursed. Something he'd been doing a lot of lately, but he might do a lot more before this was over.

Elise, too.

Standing beside him in the sheriff's office, she shook her head when she looked over the report on Buddy. Her attention landed on the same thing that'd caught Colt's eye.

That Buddy had been in juvie lockup when he was fifteen for assault with a deadly weapon.

And that his cell mate had been none other than Simon Martinelli, the now-dead hit man.

"Sweet heaven," she mumbled, and she dropped down in the seat next to Colt's desk. Judging from the way she rubbed her head, it was still hurting, and this sure wouldn't help matters.

"This didn't come up during the background check I ran on him," Elise added.

"It wouldn't have," Colt assured her. "Juvenile records are sealed."

She looked up at Reed and him, volleying glances between them. No doubt wondering how they'd managed to get the records unsealed, but Colt just shrugged.

"Reed has a few connections that he uses on occasions like this."

Reed nodded. "After the stunt Buddy pulled vandalizing your place, I thought it was strange that he didn't have a record. So, I kept digging."

And the digging had paid off. It'd given them a direct connection between Buddy and Martinelli. But there was just one problem with that.

Buddy was nowhere to be found.

The moment Reed had told him what was in the report, Colt had gone after Buddy, but the man had practically disappeared. There was an APB out on him, though, and Colt figured he would show up sooner or later. He just hoped that Buddy didn't show up around Elise. She'd already been through more than enough.

That blasted kiss included.

She darn sure didn't need any more complications to her life, but Colt had added a big one by kissing her. Twice! Heck, he'd added a big complication for himself, too, because now he was personally involved in something and with someone he shouldn't be. Especially considering he had so many other things that should be holding his attention.

"We'll find Buddy," Colt told her. "In the meantime, we'll keep searching for proof that he's the one who hired Martinelli. Unless Martinelli owed Buddy a huge favor and worked free, we might be able to get a court order and find a money trail for payment."

Elise lifted her head, looked at him. "Buddy has money. About a hundred thousand dollars. It's an account in his late mother's name, but since he was on the account, he still draws funds from it. The last time I checked, he'd withdrawn thirteen hundred."

Now it was Reed and Colt's turn to look at her. "I have connections that I use on occasions like this," she repeated.

"Legal connections?" Colt pressed.

She stared at him. "You really want to know?"

He groaned. Colt didn't mind her bending the law but not in this case. "If it's legal, we can skip the court order and try to connect that money to Martinelli."

"You'll need that court order," she confirmed. "The source I used won't own up to helping me. It wasn't illegal. Not exactly," Elise added in a mumble. "But my source could have cut a few corners."

Great. So now they needed to go about this in a way where they could actually build a case against Buddy.

"Thirteen hundred," Reed said. "That's not a big sum for a hit man, but killers have been hired for less."

Colt didn't like the way that caused Elise to cringe, but this was possibly a piece of evidence that could end in Buddy's arrest and put a stop to the danger. Not just for Elise but for his father. If Buddy had indeed done this, then it would clear his father's name.

About this, anyway.

They'd still have to deal with Elise's testimony, but Colt decided to take on one battle at a time.

Battles that involved keeping his mouth away from Elise's.

"I need to call Cooper," Colt said, taking out his phone. "He's at the county jail right now where the FBI's about to start questioning my dad."

"I'll do that for you," Reed volunteered. He tipped his head to the two messages that were waiting on Colt's desk. "You need to call them back."

Colt had already glanced at the message on top. It was from the Texas Rangers, and he was supposed to contact them with a time and place for them to take over protection detail for Elise. She glanced at the message, too, her eyebrow lifting, and Colt was about to make that call when he looked at the next message.

It was from Robert Joplin with a message to contact him ASAP.

"Did Joplin say what he wanted?" Colt asked.

Reed glanced at Elise. "Joplin made her an appointment to see a hypnotist this morning. So he can find out what else she remembers about what she saw at the cabin."

At best, the timing sucked. At worst, it was flat-out dangerous for Elise to be going to any appointments. With Buddy's money and criminal connections, he could simply hire another hit man to come after her.

Or come after her himself.

Either way, Colt didn't want to make this easier for him, and having Elise out and about was a good way to do that.

"Joplin's pressing hard," Reed commented, and he stepped aside to make the call to Cooper.

Colt hoped that pressing hard was all the man was doing. "Joplin's already put in for a mistrial, and he's looking for anything to clear Jewell's name. *Anything*," he repeated under his breath.

Elise stared at him. "Not *that*."

It was spooky that they were on the same wavelength. Of course, Colt hadn't bothered to hide his disdain for Jewell's lawyer since the man seemed hell-bent on pinning the murder charge on anyone but his client.

"Why not?" Colt asked.

She huffed and got to her feet. "Because I refuse to believe that Joplin would have me murdered all for the sake of getting a mistrial."

"Maybe murder wasn't the plan. Not your murder, anyway. He could have hired Martinelli to run you off the road but not kill you. It would have accomplished the same thing—it would have made it look as if me or someone in my family was trying to obstruct justice. Then he could have eliminated Martinelli."

Obviously being on the same wavelength didn't mean Elise agreed with him. "Joplin has never said or done anything threatening toward me. Now you think he's capable of murder?"

"Murdering a piece of scum like Martinelli—yes. And he'd be saving his client in the process."

Of course, Elise could have been seriously hurt. Or worse.

"It would also explain why Martinelli didn't just shoot you when he ran you off the road," Colt added. "And Joplin could have had those explosives set to make sure that Martinelli never told anyone who hired him."

She was shaking her head before he even finished, but the head shaking stopped, and she sank down into the chair again. "You believe Joplin could do this because he's in love with Jewell."

Oh, yeah. "They were high school sweethearts, and from everything I've heard, he didn't take it too well when she dumped him to marry my dad. He could see this as his chance to get her back and get my dad out of the picture."

Elise didn't jump to deny that. She sat there, obviously giving his theory plenty of thought. "Still, it would mean he committed murder."

Okay, so there was the denial, after all. Except she did take several more moments to think about it. "I'll call Joplin and have him cancel the appointment with the hypnotist," Elise finally said, reaching for the phone.

Good. At a minimum, it would keep her away from Joplin until Colt had more time to get to the bottom of this. And just in case it was Buddy behind the situation and not Joplin, canceling the appointment would also keep her from going someplace where she'd be easy pickings for another hit man.

Elise and Reed started their calls, and Colt was about to press in the number for the Rangers when he spotted a tall, thin woman making a beeline for the sheriff's office. Elise obviously noticed her, too, because she quickly ended the call with Joplin and got to her feet.

"You know her?" Colt immediately asked.

She pulled back her shoulders. "We haven't met, but I recognize her from her pictures. That's Meredith Darrow."

The woman Elise had recently run a background check on. A less-than-favorable one from what Elise had told him, but Meredith wasn't supposed to know about that report for another couple of days.

Judging from her tight expression, the woman had learned early. Colt figured her coming here wasn't a coincidence.

Meredith stepped inside, unwinding a pricey-looking scarf from her neck and removing her equally pricey-looking shades. Her gaze landed on him, and his badge, before her frosty green eyes went to Elise.

"Elise Nichols, I presume," Meredith said, her voice as frosty as the rest of her. Her pale blond hair, bleached-out skin and stark white coat reminded Colt of an icicle. "I drove out to your house first looking for you, and when you weren't there, I decided to come into town. Someone at the diner said they thought they'd seen you come into the sheriff's office."

Colt figured that same person could have also told

Meredith about Elise nearly being killed. Trouble of that sort didn't stay under wraps long in a small town.

"What can I do for you?" Elise asked, her tone a lot more polite than their visitor's.

"You can stop telling lies about me, that's what." Meredith shoved the shades and the scarf into her purse as if she'd declared war on them. Declared war on Elise, too.

"I don't know what you mean," Elise insisted.

"Of course you do. I read the report you sent to Frank Wellerman, the owner of the company where I applied for a job. All lies, and those lies cost me big-time. Now I could end up facing charges. I'm not going to jail because of some pencil pusher like you."

Since Colt didn't like the crazy look in Meredith's eyes, he tried to step between them, but Elise would have no part of that. Even though she obviously wasn't feeling well enough to be standing toe-to-toe with this irate woman.

"They weren't lies," Elise answered. "I was very careful and thorough with my research. I'd be happy to go over each area with you. In private."

"You think I care if this cowboy cop knows the lies you told about me? I don't," Meredith snapped. "I only want you to call Frank Wellerman and tell him that it was all a mistake. That you gave him the wrong report. Then he'll back off, and I won't end up facing charges."

"It wasn't a mistake." Elise paused. "And how'd you get the report, anyway? Mr. Wellerman assured me that he wouldn't talk to you about this until Monday, two days from now."

Meredith's chin came up. "It doesn't matter how I found out."

Which meant the woman had likely done some

hacking or at least something unethical to get her hands on that report.

"All that matters is this situation will be corrected *now*," Meredith insisted. "And you'll be the one correcting it."

Colt had heard enough of these threats. "What exactly do you think Elise lied about?"

The woman spared him a glance but kept her attention pinned to Elise. "She claimed there were some irregularities with the accounts of my current job. There's nothing wrong with those accounts. Then she implied the so-called missing funds might be linked to my brother."

"Leo Darrow," Elise explained to Colt. "He has a criminal record under an alias. I found it and included it in my report since Leo's record is for misappropriation of funds and embezzlement."

"You had no right to dig into his past," Meredith insisted.

"But I did. Companies pay me to be thorough." Elise looked at Colt. "I thought it was a red flag that her brother has been trying to do business with Frank Wellerman's company for months now but has never been able to get his foot in the door. I was concerned that maybe he was using his sister to help with that."

Meredith stabbed a perfectly manicured nail in Elise's direction. "Leo served his time, and you should have never brought him into this. *Never!*"

Since Elise had already admitted that she bent the law when searching financials, Colt didn't ask her how she'd gotten the information on Meredith. Besides, he had a bigger fish to fry.

"Someone ran Elise off the road last night," Colt tossed out there. "What do you know about that?"

Meredith made a sound of outrage.

"Well?" he pressed.

"I know nothing about it, and I resent the implication that I had anything to do with that."

"Yeah, yeah," he grumbled and turned back to Elise. "Does the ice princess have the funds to hire someone to do some dirty work?"

"She does," Elise answered without hesitation.

Colt nodded and made sure the stare he aimed at Meredith was all lawman. "Then I'm going to ask if you knew a man named Simon Martinelli?"

"Of course not." Meredith didn't hesitate, either, but again that didn't prove she was telling the truth.

"I'll do some checking," Reed volunteered. "I'll see if there's a connection, and if there is, I'll arrest you."

That clearly didn't please Meredith. "I'll be back with my lawyer, but I'm warning you, you'd better back off. I'm obviously not the only one you've managed to upset. Well, it serves you right."

Elise shook her head. "What do you mean?"

Colt wanted to know the same darn thing.

"I saw your barn," Meredith said as if that explained everything.

"You mean the red-paint splatter?" Colt asked.

"Splatter?" Meredith repeated, shaking her head. "This was more than just that. Judging from what I saw, someone obviously wants you dead."

Chapter Seven

Elise dreaded what she would see when she got home. Of course, with everything else that'd happened, nothing should surprise her. However, she figured there was plenty that could make her even more afraid than she was now.

And angry.

She was sick of feeling like the victim. Sick of having someone throw her life into upheaval this way. And especially sick of having to rely on Colt. Yet here he was again, driving her home to face heaven knew what.

Meredith had said there were death threats scrawled on the barn. Better than having someone try to run her off the road, but it was still another attempt to upset her and maybe try to force her to leave town.

"Thank you for doing this," she mumbled to Colt.

"No need to thank me. No way would I have let you come back out here by yourself."

Nor would Elise have come alone. As sick and angry as she was about the incidents, she wasn't stupid and didn't want to make herself an easy target for another attack, and coming alone would have done just that.

Colt glanced at her, but then he continued those lawman glimpses all around them. No doubt making sure that someone wasn't following them. Elise was trying to make sure of that, too, because after all, someone could have used this as a ruse to get them back out in the open. That's the reason that Reed was following behind them in his truck. That, and because they weren't sure what they were about to face when she got home.

The death-threat graffiti might not be all they'd have to deal with.

There could be someone waiting to try to kill her.

And that brought her right back to their suspects.

"Buddy could have made a return visit," she said. In fact, he was the most likely candidate since he'd already vandalized the barn once.

Colt made a sound of agreement. "We'll find him, question him. We'll also question Meredith again since she admitted to being out here."

Yet something else that was unnerving. The woman obviously despised her and had come all the way out to her home to threaten her. Of course, that led Elise to the next thought.

"If Meredith did this, wouldn't she know she'd be an automatic suspect?" she asked.

"Yeah, but she might have seen the other paint splatter and thought she could blame it on someone else. A sort of reverse psychology."

True. "Joplin might be trying to use reverse psychology, as well. Especially since this wasn't a physical threat against me." But she hated to think that Jewell's lawyer or anyone else would go to such extremes. Of course, someone had gone to an even bigger extreme than this by hiring a hit man.

Elise paused. "Do you think anyone in Whitt Braddock's family could be behind all this?"

Colt shrugged. "I don't see why. His wife and kids probably don't care who's convicted for his death. They just want justice. None of them have said a thing about you returning to testify for Jewell."

She had to agree with that, and a mistrial was the last thing they'd want. If fact, Whitt's family might be glad that her testimony could implicate Whitt's old nemesis, Roy McKinnon.

So, they were back to Joplin, Buddy or Meredith. Elise hoped they were the only ones on her list but maybe not. What if the culprit was someone else? Perhaps someone from her past.

Some former potential employees she'd given an unfavorable report and who was now out for revenge?

She made a mental note to go through her old files and see if there was something she'd missed. Over the years, there had been a few people who'd gotten angry that she'd uncovered something unsavory about them, but no motive for murder immediately came to mind. And she was pretty sure she would have remembered something like that.

Colt checked the time. "The Ranger should be here within an hour or so. We'll work out the details of where you're going then."

Because she had so much on her mind, it took a moment for that to sink in. Those *details* with the Ranger likely wouldn't involve Colt staying with her. That should have pleased her. And it would have done just that twenty-four hours earlier.

Not now, though.

"You're uncomfortable around me because of the kiss," she admitted, even though she figured it was a subject Colt would want to avoid.

He did. The sudden tightening of his jaw confirmed that. "I'm uncomfortable around *me* because of the kiss. Because it shouldn't have happened." He cursed. "Us getting involved would be the worst idea in the history of bad ideas."

She couldn't argue with that. His father and brothers probably hated her, and she was the last person on earth they'd want around Colt. Plus, she didn't think it was her imagination that Colt was still holding a grudge for her leaving all those years ago.

Or not.

A grudge would have meant that he'd actually had feelings for her that went beyond a teenage crush. He certainly hadn't said a word to stop her when she'd brought up the subject of leaving Sweetwater Springs to go to college in Dallas instead of heading to the University of Texas where he was going.

Not. A. Word.

Okay, so maybe Colt wasn't the only one holding on to a grudge here. A grudge still mixed with attraction.

Yes, nothing could go wrong with that combination.

"We can just agree that the kiss was a mistake," she said, "and that it won't happen again."

Colt gave her a flat look. "If we're around each other, it'll happen again."

She returned the flat look. Or rather tried. "It won't happen again," she repeated, hoping if she said it enough, it would come true.

Or at least it might want her to make it come true.

"It'll happen," he argued. His gaze went from her mouth to her breasts. "And next time, it might not just stay a kiss."

Oh, that really didn't help. The look alone had caused her to go all warm and golden, and the thought of pushing this further took her well past the warmth stage and made her forget all sorts of things.

Like the grudge. And common sense.

At least for several moments.

Then Colt took the final turn for her place, and the house and barn came into view. He slowed the truck to a crawl and put his hand over his gun. Bracing for an attack. But Elise didn't see anything that would require him to pull his weapon.

Well, other than the obscene threat scrawled in red paint on the side of her barn. And there was no doubt about it, it was a threat.

Stay here and you die.

It was surrounded by other obscenities, all obviously meant to unnerve her.

Sadly, it was working.

"Don't get out yet," Colt insisted when he brought the truck to a stop.

Cursing, he used his phone to take several pictures, but Colt didn't get out until Reed had stopped directly behind him. "Help me keep an eye on Elise," he told his fellow deputy.

He walked toward the barn, his attention still firing all around them. Reed's, too. They drew their weapons, went to the barn opening and looked inside.

Colt glanced back at her and shook his head. "No one's here."

Elise wasn't exactly relieved about that. If Colt had managed to catch the person red-handed, literally, then the danger would be over, and she might be able to get on with her life.

"I'll check the house and make sure no one broke in," Reed offered.

The deputy walked toward her front porch. Elise got out of the truck and went to stand by Colt. He opened his mouth, maybe to tell her to get back in the truck, but they both knew she wasn't necessarily any safer there than she was by the barn. After all, bullets could go through glass.

When she made it to the doorway, Elise immediately saw the spilled can of red paint. Or rather what was left of it. The person who'd written that message had used most of what remained to put that garbage on the wall.

But who had done that?

"I don't suppose a handwriting expert can figure out who wrote it?" she asked.

He lifted his shoulder. "I'll send a photo of it to the crime lab, but graffiti's hard to match. Still, we might get some prints off the paint can and the brush."

That was a start, but if they did find Buddy's prints on it, he could claim they'd gotten there from the time he'd admitted to vandalizing her barn. That left Joplin and Meredith, and neither should have been inside her barn and near that paint can.

Of course, she hadn't seen paint on Meredith's white outfit, so it if had been the woman's doing, then she'd used gloves and had avoided any splatter. Still, she didn't seem the sort of woman who'd get her hands dirty.

Colt cursed again, and Elise followed his gaze to see what had gotten his attention. There, on the inside of the wall was yet more red paint. Unlike the other warning and profanity, this appeared to be just one word, but Elise couldn't make out what it was.

She stepped closer at the same moment that Colt did, and Elise felt something bump across the front of her leg. At first she thought it was twine from an old hay bale, but she saw the sunlight glint off it.

A wire.

"Move!" Colt yelled.

There was the groaning sound of the wood as the roof collapsed and fell right toward them.

Colt hooked his arm around Elise and snapped her backward. Away from the falling wood.

It wasn't a second too soon.

The roof of the rickety barn swooshed down, one of the thick beams glancing off the toe of Colt's boot, but he managed to get Elise out of the way. He pushed her into what was left of the doorway and then outside.

And he kept going with her in tow.

He dragged them behind the first thing he reached, an old watering trough, while the rest of the barn crashed to the ground. The dust, wood bits and debris kicked up all around them.

Elise's breath was already gusting, and her eyes were wide. "There was a wire," she managed to say.

"Yeah. I saw it a little too late." And that wire meant someone had rigged the roof to fall. Probably the same person who'd written the latest rounds of threats.

"Are you okay?" Reed called out. He came from the back of Elise's house, running toward them with his gun drawn.

Colt did a quick check to make sure Elise hadn't been hurt. She was visibly shaken, but thank heaven she didn't seem to have any new injuries. They'd gotten lucky—again—and Colt hated to rely on something like luck when it came to Elise's safety.

"Someone trip-wired it," Colt let his fellow deputy know.

Reed mumbled something under his breath when he saw the pile of rubble that'd once been the barn. "I'll get someone out here," he said, stopping to take out his phone.

Good. Because they'd need help. Maybe they would be able to get something to identify the sick SOB who'd done this. It was attempted murder. Not just Elise this time but Colt, too.

Elise looked at him, her bottom lip trembling. "What was the word written on the inside wall of the barn?"

Even though it wouldn't do anything to settle her nerves, Colt opened his mouth to tell her, but he heard something that stopped him. Some kind of movement on the other side of his truck. He looked up, didn't see anything.

Then he heard the shot.

"Get down!" he shouted to Reed, but the deputy was already doing just that.

Colt's heart jumped to his throat, and he shoved Elise lower so he could shield her with his body. Thankfully, Reed was still close enough to the house that he took cover by the side of the porch.

Just as another shot came their way.

The bullet went over their heads and into the barn debris. The trough that Colt was using was cast-iron but rusted through in spots. Definitely not enough protection from bullets, but it was too risky to try to move now. Especially when the shooter fired another shot.

Hindsight being twenty-twenty, Colt knew it'd been a huge mistake to bring Elise here to her ranch. A mistake that could cost them, big-time. All he could do now was stop this idiot and beat some answers out of him.

"I'm so sorry," Elise mumbled.

He wasn't looking for an apology, especially when this wasn't her fault, but Colt couldn't take the time to reassure her. Too much of a distraction. Instead, he focused on the angle of the shots. Whoever was trying to kill them was on the far side of his truck, probably behind some trees that rimmed the fence around Elise's property.

"You see him?" Colt shouted to Reed.

"Not yet. But backup's on the way."

Colt lifted his head just a fraction to see if he could get a glimpse of the guy, but Elise pulled him right back down. "Don't," she insisted. "He could kill you."

He wasn't especially fond of the idea of risking his life, either, but the shots couldn't go on like this. Even if one didn't hit them directly, there were too many things that could cause a bullet to ricochet.

The next shot came, and it was a lightbulb-over-the-head moment for Colt. Each of the shots was aimed at the same place. Not just nearby.

But in the exact spot in what was left of the barn.

If the shooter had actually been aiming at them, the bullets would have gone into the trough. Or into him when he'd lifted his head.

"I don't think he's trying to kill us," Colt mumbled. But that didn't mean that he could just jump out there and test the theory.

"Take out my phone," he told Elise, maneuvering toward her so she could do that. "Text Reed and tell him to circle around the back of your house so he can get a look at this guy."

Even though her hands were shaking as hard as the rest of her, Elise managed to get out his phone and send the text. The shots continued, spaced out about every five seconds. All still going into the same spot.

"If someone's trying to scare me," Elise whispered, "they're doing a good job of it."

Yeah. And maybe that was the only thing this nut job had in mind. If so, it could be Buddy or Joplin. Of course, Meredith might be getting plenty of pleasure from watching Elise being too terrified to go to her own home.

His phone buzzed. Elise still had it in a death grip, but Colt managed to see the screen and the message from Reed: Spotted a rifle in the trees by the fence. Can't tell who's shooting. Moving in closer.

Colt didn't have to remind Reed to be careful. Reed was a good deputy and would be. Still, if he spooked the shooter, the guy could send some of those shots Reed's way.

Another shot came, and Colt counted off the seconds in his head. Five, just like the others. And not a degree of variation on the angle of the shot. The recoil alone should cause most shooters to move their hands just a little to throw off the individual shots so that each bullet wouldn't land in the exact spot each time.

Hell.

"Text Reed to tell him that I think the rifle's rigged to a remote control," he said to Elise.

Elise looked back at him, her eyes widening again. While she texted, she glanced at the next bullet that bashed into the heap of wood. Each new shot confirmed Colt's theory. However, that didn't mean the shooter wasn't still out there, ready to gun them down if they stepped from cover.

The seconds crawled by. The shots continued.

Colt held his breath and hoped like the devil that Reed wasn't walking into some kind of trap. Or that the shooter wasn't closing in on Elise and him now that Reed didn't have their backs. Just in case, Colt kept watch all around them.

His phone buzzed again, and Reed's message popped up: You're right. Remote control. No shooter in sight.

But unless the remote control was on a timer, the shooter would have to be close enough to operate it.

Too close, and there were plenty of places for someone to hide.

I'm moving in, Reed texted.

Colt scrambled over Elise and to the end of the watering trough so he could try to provide some backup for his fellow deputy. He immediately spotted Reed darting from one tree to the other and directly toward the fence. It seemed to take an eternity, but Colt figured it was less than a minute before Reed made it to the rifle.

The shots stopped.

"Stay down," Colt warned Elise.

Even though the bullets were no longer a danger, they were far from being safe. He levered himself up and tried to pick through the surroundings to see if he could find who'd just set this all in motion.

Nothing.

No timer, Reed texted.

So, whoever had done this had to be close. Colt couldn't go after him because he couldn't leave Elise alone, but he watched, waited. While he kept his gun ready.

Finally, he heard something. A snap. As if someone had stepped on a twig. But it hadn't come from anywhere near the disarmed rifle and Reed. It'd come from behind Elise and him. On the other side of the barn.

Colt pivoted in that direction and saw the blur of motion. Someone moving behind an old storage shed. With just that brief glimpse, he couldn't tell if it was one of their suspects or someone else.

Maybe another hired gun.

But if it was a hired gun, why hadn't he just shot them? Why had the person instead rigged a gun on the remote control?

Maybe the plan was to pin them down and then come

in for the kill. Someone who wasn't so sure of their shot might do something like that.

Colt motioned to the shed. "Text Reed again," he said to Elise. "Tell him that's the location of the person who set all of this up."

She nodded but had barely gotten started when Colt heard another sound that he definitely didn't want to hear.

Someone running.

Whoever was out there was getting away.

Chapter Eight

"This is a really bad idea," Elise mumbled.

Not her first time to mumble it, either, since they'd driven away from her house. Elise had been saying it since Colt had told her that the gunman had gotten away.

And that he was taking her to his family's ranch.

She needed protection. The latest attack had proved that. But she wasn't sure that walking into the lion's den, aka the McKinnon ranch, was the best way to make that happen.

"You know your brothers and father don't want me there," she added.

"My brothers are at work, and my sister Rayanne and her husband are at a doctor's appointment in San Antonio."

That still left his father.

"Maybe the Rangers can find a different place to take me," she added.

Colt didn't say a word, but the glance he gave her said loads. She wasn't going anywhere with anybody until they got to the bottom of this.

Whatever *this* was.

Someone had rigged that barn to fall on them. Perhaps like the shots from the rifle being controlled remotely, it'd only been meant to scare her and get her running.

But why?

Did that mean her attacker hadn't wanted to kill her? Or maybe he hadn't wanted to get close enough to try to kill her with Colt around.

Part of her wanted to do just that—run. But the other part of her hated that someone was trying to force her out of her home. Maybe force her from testifying against Roy, too.

Which led Elise to repeat her mumble about this being a bad idea.

"Your father won't want me at the ranch," she reminded him. And she wouldn't blame him one bit. In this case, the truth wasn't going to set him free. Just the opposite. It didn't matter that she was in the middle of a fight for her life. Technically, Roy McKinnon was, too.

A muscle flickered in Colt's jaw. "You won't have to stay long. Just while I set up a safe house. I figured it was better to come here since it's closer than going back to the sheriff's office."

Where they could be attacked again on the drive over.

Of course, they could be attacked anywhere, including his family's ranch.

That was no doubt the reason Colt was keeping a vigilant watch all around them. Elise was, too, and she wondered just how long it would take her to stop looking over her shoulder.

A long time, especially if the attacks continued.

The only way they would stop was for them to find the person responsible and put him or her behind bars, but they seemed no closer to making that happen than when this had first started.

"Reed and Cooper will keep looking for the shooter," Colt continued. "And there might be some prints or something on the rifle and the stand. We might even be able to find the remote control he was using."

Elise knew that Colt's brother and Reed were good lawmen and would do their best, but their attacker had headed straight for the woods. Hard to find someone in there if they didn't want to be found. Besides, the guy probably had an escape plan in place before the attack even started.

"What about the barn?" she asked.

He paused a moment as if gathering his thoughts. "It wouldn't have been hard to set a trip wire to bring down an old barn like that. But the person would have needed some time to do it."

She shuddered because that likely meant someone had sneaked onto her land during the night or had done it while they were at the sheriff's office. And that led Elise to her next question.

"Would Buddy have had time when he went up in the hayloft to get that box?" she asked.

"Not really. He was only in there a couple of minutes, and it would have taken more time than that to brace those rafters to be brought down by a trip wire." He paused, groaned and wearily scrubbed his hand over his face.

"What is it?" she pressed.

"Buddy could have already had everything in place before he showed up. Maybe things he'd put in place on another visit. If so, he wouldn't have needed much time to string the wire onto whatever he'd rigged to bring down the roof."

She didn't have any idea of the mechanics of such a thing, but Buddy knew every inch of that barn. Of all their suspects, he would have known the best way to orchestrate this particular attack. He would have also had the easiest time sneaking onto the ranch since he no doubt knew the trails on the property.

It sickened her to think that Buddy would do something that could have killed them, but then he'd been nothing but hostile to her since her return. It didn't take much to believe that he could have escalated things with the booby trap and then the shots.

So, the culprit could have indeed been Buddy. In fact, as far as she was concerned, he was number one on their list of suspects.

"What was written on the wall?" she asked when Colt didn't continue.

She braced herself to hear yet another threat or warning for her to get out of town, but Colt's silence had her turning in the seat to face him. "What was it?" Elise pressed.

"It said 'For Roy.'"

It took her a moment to realize what that meant. Another moment for it to hit her like a punch to the stomach.

Elise pressed her fingers to her mouth. "Oh, God."

"It doesn't mean anything," Colt quickly said. "Buddy could have put it there to take suspicion off him. Meredith and Joplin, too."

He was right, of course, but it didn't make this easier to swallow, especially since they were so close to a meeting that she didn't want to have. Colt took the turn to his family's ranch where she would no doubt come face-to-face with Roy McKinnon, the very man that her testimony would implicate in a murder.

Of course, Roy's name on the wall implicated him in some way in the attacks against her. Or rather it implicated someone who wanted to protect him.

"This is a bad idea," she repeated—again.

"I called ahead. They know you're coming."

That didn't help, either. It also didn't help when Elise saw the woman standing on the porch.

Colt's sister Rosalie.

Once Elise and she had been childhood friends despite the three-year age difference between them, and while Rosalie had welcomed Elise's testimony so that it'd clear her mother's name, Elise still wasn't sure of the reception she'd get. From all accounts, Rosalie had reconciled with her father, so Elise braced herself for a frosty welcome.

That didn't happen.

Rosalie came down the porch steps when Elise got out of the truck, and immediately pulled her into her arms. "I'm so sorry. Are you both okay?" she asked, volleying glances between Elise and her brother.

Elise managed a nod and was feeling a little better about this visit. Until she spotted Roy in the doorway, that is.

"Dad," Colt greeted him. "You remember Elise."

"Of course." The corner of his weathered mouth lifted into what she thought might be a welcoming smile. "Sorry about the trouble you're having."

He sounded genuine enough, but Elise didn't expect to get the warm, fuzzy feeling that she'd just gotten from Rosalie.

Colt looped his arm around Elise's waist and got her moving up the steps. Good thing, too, because she no longer felt steady on her feet. "Elise just needs a place to rest and wait until I've made other arrangements."

His father nodded. "She's welcome here anytime. And for as long as she needs." His gaze came to hers. "I was sorry to hear of your grandmother's passing. She was a good woman."

Elise somehow got her mouth working and thanked him, and Roy stepped to the side, motioning for her to go in. She did, with Colt and Rosalie trailing right along behind her.

"The guest room's ready for you," Rosalie said, but she immediately stopped when she heard a baby fussing. "That's Sadie, my daughter, and she's obviously not happy with her lunch. I need to go and help Mary."

Elise didn't need an explanation as to who Mary was. She'd been a housekeeper at the McKinnon ranch for as long as Elise could remember. Yet someone else that she had fond memories of from childhood. Too bad all those memories didn't ease the discomfort she was feeling now.

"I'll be up to check on you later," Rosalie added. She hurried away, leaving Roy, Colt and her in an uneasy silence.

"You might have heard that Rosalie's getting married," Roy commented. "He's a good man. Rayanne's husband, too."

Thanks to the town gossips, Elise had caught up on the McKinnons. All of Colt's siblings were either married or engaged now and settling into a normal life. Well, as normal as life could be with their mother's murder trial hanging over their heads.

Even though the conversation was civil enough, Colt must have picked up on the fact that she was well past the awkward stage, because he took her by the arm. "This way," he said, glancing back at his dad. "Thanks."

Elise thanked him, too, and made her way up the stairs with Colt. She remembered this part of the house, had even done a sleepover with Rosalie when they were kids. Right before Whitt Braddock had gone missing and Rosalie's world had crashed down around her.

Colt's world, too.

After the scandal and rumors of her murdering her lover, his mother had left with his twin sisters and had started the bad blood that she could still feel twenty-three years later. It didn't matter that everyone had gotten on with their lives. Well, for a while, anyway. Until Jewell's arrest.

And Elise remembering the events of that tragic day.

Colt took her to the room at the end of the hall. Once this had been Jewell's sewing room, but now it was a guest bedroom decorated in dark browns and creams like the rest of the house. No trace of Jewell or the life that'd once gone on here.

"I'm sorry to put you through this," Colt mumbled.

"I'm sorry to put you through this," she repeated right back to him.

The corner of his mouth lifted, but the smile didn't make it to his eyes. Because he looked in worse shape than she felt, Elise reached out, pulled him to her. She felt his back muscles stiffen, and for a moment she thought he might pull away. But he didn't.

"Hugging is the last thing we should be doing," he reminded her. "That goes for touching, standing close to each other or even thinking about doing any of those things."

True. But that didn't stop her.

Being with him like this pushed aside the sound of those gunshots and the other attack. Somewhat of a miracle. But Elise knew it couldn't last. Still, she held on, needing this from him.

Colt must have needed it, too, because he put his arm around her, tugged her closer and closer until they were right against each other.

That helped distract her despite his warning that they shouldn't be doing this.

And so did the touch of his mouth when he brushed it over her lips. Very chaste. At first, anyway.

Colt made a groaning sound that rumbled deep in his chest, and he deepened the kiss. That really helped with the nightmarish images, and they faded fast, replaced by the instant heat that the kiss created.

Elise hooked her arms around his neck. Anchoring him against her. And she let that heat warm her in all the cold places. Soon, though, the warmth got much hotter when he pressed her against the door, closing it at the same time that he snapped her to him.

"Yes," she mumbled against his mouth.

But Colt certainly wasn't saying yes. She could feel the fight going on inside him. His muscles were corded. His heartbeat fast and wild. Like the kiss itself and the body contact.

Even though at least one of them should have had the good sense to back away, that didn't happen. Hard for good sense to prevail, though, when his kisses brought back the flood of emotions that she'd been trying to bury for the past decade.

Colt had had her hormonal number back then. And he still had it now.

The kiss raged on, but it didn't take long until it wasn't enough. Her body begged for more, and even though she didn't ask, Colt figured it out and gave her more. He aligned their bodies so that the front of his jeans was against hers.

"Yes," Elise repeated.

It was exactly what her body wanted. What she needed. But it was also something that shouldn't be happening. Not right now, anyway.

Did that stop them?

No.

But the knock on the door certainly did.

Groaning again, Colt moved away from her. "Yeah?" he managed to say, though his breath was gusting.

"Sorry to bother you," Rosalie said from the other side of the door. "But Elise has a visitor waiting on the front porch. It's Robert Joplin, and he's not alone. There's a man named Tim Sutcliff with him."

Colt looked at her, questioning whether she knew who that was. She didn't. But with the stunt that Joplin was trying with the mistrial, there was no telling who this other man could be.

"A couple of the ranch hands came to the porch when Joplin arrived," Rosalie went on. "They're armed and said you gave them orders to keep an eye out for him or anyone else who might show up while Elise was here."

Colt had indeed done that with a phone call he'd made on the drive out to the ranch.

"I'll be down in a few minutes," Colt answered. "Don't let Joplin in the house. Keep him on the porch with the ranch hands."

Rosalie paused, maybe waiting for an explanation, but finally said, "Okay."

Colt paused, too, his gaze combing over Elise, and then he cursed, shook his head. "We look like we just had sex."

Elise couldn't help it. She laughed. And because she thought they both could use it, she brushed a kiss on his cheek. A chaste one like Colt's that had started this whole kissing session.

"Well, for years I did dream about having sex with you," she admitted.

He'd already reached to open the door, but that stopped him. "You did?"

Elise nearly blurted out that she'd been attracted to Colt since the first moment she realized the difference between boys and girls. Before that, he'd been her friend. Yes, she'd had a thing for Colt McKinnon most of her life.

"You used to kill spiders for me in my tree house," she settled for saying. "Those kinds of heroics stay with a girl."

"Killing spiders, huh?" He shook his head. "That's what it took to be a hero in your eyes?"

"It's helped."

Despite their visitor, and their messy situation, they shared a smile. Too brief. Because then Colt opened the door, stepping in front of her.

"I don't want you near Joplin," he reminded her as they went downstairs. He was all lawman now. Ready to stomp on more spiders for her if necessary. "Stay in the foyer while I talk to him."

Elise didn't argue, mainly because she didn't especially want to see Joplin after the hellish day she'd had. However, she did want to know why he was there, so she stayed just inside the doorway when Colt opened the door.

Rosalie stepped next to her, standing shoulder to shoulder with her. That's when Elise realized Rosalie was holding a gun by her side. Obviously, she, too, thought there might be reason for concern. And maybe there was. After all, someone had attempted to hurt her twice in the past twenty-four hours.

"Colt," Joplin greeted, but there was no friendliness to it. The man hitched his thumb to the pair of ranch hands who were clearly guarding him from each side of the porch. "Is this necessary?"

"Yeah," Colt answered without hesitation. "We're a little tired of dodging bullets and falling barn roofs. How'd you even know Elise was here and what do you want?"

Those brusque questions didn't ease the tightness around Joplin's mouth. "When she wasn't at the sheriff's office, I figured you'd bring her here." He stepped to the side so that Colt and she would get a good look at the man he'd brought with him.

Tim Sutcliff was short and stocky with bushy brown hair. He gave his thick wool coat an adjustment so that it hugged the back of his neck. He was obviously cold, but Elise knew that wouldn't gain him or Joplin entry to the house.

"Mr. Sutcliff is a therapist," Joplin explained. "He's here to hypnotize Elise to see what else she remembers about that day she saw Roy in the Braddock cabin."

Elise wasn't sure who groaned louder. Colt or her.

"This can wait," Colt insisted.

"No, it can't. At the rate things are going, Elise might not live long enough to testify about what she saw."

Even though she wasn't standing directly in the gusting wind, that chilled her to the bone. Because it was true. And it might be true because of Joplin.

"Please tell me you didn't have anything to do with what's been happening to me," Elise said.

Oh, Joplin did not like that. But she didn't care. She wasn't especially fond of what had gone on, either, and right now, Joplin had a strong motive for the attacks against her.

"I wouldn't hurt you," Joplin snapped. "I'm trying to help you. Don't you want to remember that day?"

"Of course I do, but I'm not sure you have my best interests at heart." Something that'd taken her a while to figure out, but she certainly had it figured out now. Joplin's first and foremost concern was Jewell.

Elise's gaze shifted to the therapist. "Let me guess—you and Joplin are friends?"

The man opened his mouth, sputtering out a few frustrated sounds, before he answered, "That has nothing to do with your situation. Like Robert, I only want to help you."

"Robert," she repeated in a mumble. "I'd say that's the answer to my question, that you two are indeed friends."

Sutcliff shook his head. "Again, that has nothing to do with anything. I'm here to help you," he repeated.

"It has everything to do with this situation," Colt argued. "If Elise wants to see a hypnotist, then it should be someone she chooses. Someone who's not a friend of my mother's attorney."

Neither Joplin nor Sutcliff actually denied the friendship, but both look riled to the core. "Why would it make a difference if we happen to know each other?" Joplin challenged.

"I can think of a reason," Rosalie said before Colt or Elise could answer. "A dishonest or untrained therapist can plant false memories in a person while they're under hypnosis. Memories that you might use to clear your client."

Colt gave her an odd look, maybe because he was surprised that Rosalie wouldn't do anything and everything to clear her mother's name. "I only want to know the truth," Rosalie explained. "And I don't want Elise bullied into doing something she's not ready to do.

Especially by someone who might not even be qualified to do it."

"Thank you," Elise told her and then turned back to Joplin. "I'll make my own appointment to see a hypnotist, and no offense, Mr. Sutcliff, but it won't be with you."

She didn't think it was her imagination that Sutcliff seemed extremely uncomfortable about her decision. Had Joplin pressured his old friend to do something illegal? Probably. Joplin was pulling out the stops when it came to this trial.

"You don't trust me," Joplin said to her, his voice low and filled with emotion. Well, one emotion, anyway. Anger.

"No, I don't," Elise readily admitted.

Joplin's nostrils actually flared. "This is a bad decision on your part. I'll petition the court to have you removed from Colt's protective custody."

"Good luck with that," Colt grumbled, obviously not overly concerned about that happening.

Still, Joplin could make waves, and that was all the more reason for her to get to a safe house where Joplin couldn't just show up on a whim. Of course, that safe house might come with a huge string attached.

Colt might not be there with her.

In fact, after that latest kiss—which he would see as another lapse in judgment—he might try to distance himself from her. Something that Elise figured was best overall. But it certainly didn't feel best at the moment.

"I've also secured the Braddock cabin where Whitt was killed," Joplin went on. "There's a guard with the private investigators that I hired."

It took Elise a moment to realize why Joplin had said that. Colt obviously got it right away because he huffed.

"My family and I have no intention of tampering with a crime scene," Colt informed him.

"Maybe not," Joplin said, speaking over his shoulder as he walked away. "But I'm removing the temptation just in case somebody puts something there that'd clear Roy's name at the expense of your mother."

Elise thought that part might be directed at her. Probably because she'd already admitted that she didn't trust Joplin, he might think that mistrust extended to Jewell. It didn't. She wanted to help the woman if she was indeed innocent.

"I don't think you've seen the last of him," Rosalie mumbled as they went back inside. All three of them stayed at the window to make sure Joplin and Sutcliff got in their car and drove away.

"It's true about someone being able to plant false memories?" Colt asked his sister.

Rosalie nodded. "It's especially easy to do with childhood memories. Some therapists have even convinced people they were molested and such when it didn't happen."

Mercy, and Joplin could have planned on doing that to her so that she believed Roy had been the one to kill Whitt Braddock.

And he might have been.

Even though her memories weren't crystal clear, Elise was certain about one thing. Roy had been at the cabin that day.

Rosalie gave her arm a gentle squeeze. "I know someone reputable who can do the hypnosis, and I can get you an appointment with her. But if you'd rather use someone else, I'll understand."

"No. Please make the appointment," Elise insisted. "If you trust her, then so do I."

Rosalie looked at Colt to see what he thought about it, and he nodded. "Thanks. For everything," he added.

"Yes," someone said.

Elise looked behind them and spotted Roy standing in the shadows of the adjoining family room. He came closer, his worn cowboy boots thudding on the hardwood floor, his hands jammed into his jeans' pockets.

"I don't know what you're going to remember while under hypnosis," he said. "But even if you saw something that leads to my arrest, I don't want you to hold back." His gaze drifted to Colt. "In fact, I don't want anything you remember to have any bearing on anything else."

Elise understood then. Roy could no doubt see the attraction simmering between Colt and her. Heck, it'd always been there, and it was getting stronger. Roy didn't want her feelings for Colt playing into her testimony.

And it wouldn't.

Still, she hated the thought of remembering something that might make all this worse for Roy, even if it made things better for Jewell.

"Who knows," Elise said, "I might remember someone else being in the cabin that day. Someone else who had a reason to harm Whitt Braddock."

There was no shortage of people who fell into that category. Even as a child, she'd known that Whitt wasn't a well-liked man, and his supposed affair with Jewell, a married woman, certainly hadn't helped his reputation any. Too bad all those people had airtight alibis, putting the blame squarely back on Jewell and Roy.

Colt drew in a long breath and made another check to ensure that Joplin had driven away. He had. And he took out his phone. "I'll check on the status of the safe house."

However, his phone buzzed before he could make a

call, and Elise saw Reed's name on the screen. Since the deputy was likely still at her place, she prayed that he'd found something to lead them to the identity of the person who'd launched the attacks on Colt and her.

Colt answered the call but didn't put it on speaker. Still, it didn't take Elise long to realize that something bad had happened. She groaned because she was tired of having this constant dose of bad news.

"Get in here, away from the windows," Colt insisted. He took her by the arm and hurried her into the family room.

That caused the skin to crawl on Elise's neck.

Mercy, what had gone wrong now?

Rosalie had a similar reaction. "My baby," she said on a rise of breath, and she raced off toward the back of the house.

"It's Buddy," Colt said the moment he finished the call with Reed. And he drew his gun. "He was just spotted on the road leading to the ranch."

Chapter Nine

"You should try to get some rest," Colt reminded Elise.

But it was a reminder that fell on deaf ears because Elise continued to pace back and forth across the family room while they waited for yet another call from Reed. Colt hoped this one would be to tell them that Buddy had been captured. Putting Buddy behind bars might not be the end of their problems, but at least he could question the man and find out why he was on the run.

Innocent men didn't usually run, and he was betting that Buddy had something to do with not only the barn falling but possibly the other attacks, as well.

"How long before your brothers get home?" Elise asked, glancing out the window again.

Well, glancing as much as she could, considering Colt had warned her to stay far away from the windows and doors. It was a necessity since shots from a long-range rifle could be fired at them from the woods across from the ranch. The ranch hands were all on alert, looking for anyone who might try to get close to launch an attack, but the ranch was huge and there was a lot of ground to cover.

"How long?" she repeated when he didn't answer.

He lifted his shoulder. "Don't worry. They won't come here. Cooper built a house in that clearing near

the pond, and Tucker lives just up the road in my grand-
daddy's old place. Besides, Tucker and his wife took
their twins on a family vacation."

The only McKinnon sibling that Elise might have to
face was his other sister, Rayanne, but Rosalie had already called Rayanne and asked that she and her husband stay in a hotel in San Antonio. With Rayanne being
nearly six months pregnant, it was just too risky for her
to return to the ranch.

Risky for Elise to be there, too, so Colt made yet another call so he could get an update about the safe house.
The Ranger in charge didn't answer, and Colt left him
a message. However, he'd no sooner done that when a
text message popped onto his screen.

Colt cursed.

That definitely wasn't what he wanted to hear from
Reed—that there was no sign of Buddy by the time the
deputy had made it out to the road where the man had
been spotted by a neighbor.

"Buddy got away," Elise concluded, and groaning,
she dropped down on the sofa next to him.

"Yes," Colt confirmed. "For now, anyway. There are
a lot of people looking for him, and the Appaloosa Pass
Sheriff's Office has helped us set up a roadblock to help
catch him. Buddy can't hide forever." He hoped. "Don't
worry. The safe house should be ready soon."

But, of course, she'd worry. So would he. Every second felt like a time bomb clicking down to explosion.

And that wasn't just about the danger.

It was about all this heat sizzling and crackling between them. The timing for it sucked, not just because
of her testimony, but also because attraction equaled
a distraction, and something like that could get them
killed. His family killed, too.

Another text message popped up, this one from Rosalie. "My sister scheduled you an appointment tomorrow morning with Suzanne Dawkins, the hypnotist."

Elise nodded. "Is it safe for me to go and see her?"

At this point Colt wasn't sure what was safe, but at least the appointment might give them some answers. Hopefully, one of those answers would help clear his father's name.

Colt went over Rosalie's text again. "According to what Rosalie's saying, the hypnotist will come to you, but since you'll be in the safe house by then, it's probably best if we go to the sheriff's office for the session. I want as few people as possible to know the location of the safe house."

She nodded again, stared at her hands. "You won't be staying there with me, will you?"

It was something Colt had gone over more than a dozen times in his mind, and he still didn't have an answer. He shouldn't stay with her, especially since he had a mountain of deputy work he should be doing. Also, he had obviously lost objectivity when it came to Elise, but he wasn't sure he was ready to turn her over to the Rangers.

Of course, the lost objectivity was coloring that last concern, too.

Another lawman could protect her, but he wasn't sure he wanted to give up that duty to someone else.

So, the argument inside him continued.

"We'll see," he settled for saying.

And he hated how unsure that sounded, but his final decision would come after he had a better idea of the arrangements the Rangers were making for her. If he felt that the safe house was truly the safest place to be, then he'd back off. No matter how hard it would be for him to do that.

"I'd like to go by my place and pick up some things before I go to the safe house," she said.

He shook his head. "I can have someone do that for you."

"I'd like to do it myself." And the color rose on her cheeks enough to get his full attention. His attention was enough to cause her to huff, though. "I don't want strangers going through my underwear drawer." She paused. "Plus, I need to get my meds."

Again, she got his attention. "Are you in pain?" he asked, glancing at the stitches still on her head. Now that she'd taken off the bandage, they were easy to see.

Another huff. "I need to get my birth control pills, all right?"

Oh. That. Colt kicked himself for not picking up on the fact she might need personal items that she didn't want to discuss with him. Then he kicked himself again for feeling that tug of jealousy that she'd need such a thing.

Hell.

What was wrong with him? Elise and he were on totally separate paths, and those paths would get significantly further apart if her testimony put his father behind bars. Plus, it was reasonable that an attractive woman like her would have a man in her life. A man who would require her to be on the pill.

Yet another pang of jealousy hit him before Colt could shove it away.

"There hasn't been anyone in a while," Elise said, no doubt reading his expression. "But I stay on them. Habit, I guess."

Colt didn't want to be relieved by that, but he was.

He quickly assured himself that it was because adding someone else—*anyone* else—into this mix would complicate things even more. It had nothing to do with those two scalding-hot kisses Elise and he had shared.

Okay, it did.

But Colt didn't intend to let those kisses play into this.

"I'd rather not ask someone to pick up my personal things," she added. "I'd like to go by my place for just a couple of minutes. Unless you think there might be other booby traps?"

"No. A couple of the deputies from Appaloosa Pass went over every inch of your place. If there were other trip wires or such, they would have found them."

"So we can go," she concluded.

His first instinct was still to say no, but the truth was, whoever was behind all this was just as likely to attack at the ranch as Elise's house. In fact, he probably should get her away from Rosalie and his niece—especially since Rosalie's fiancé was away on business and couldn't help protect her. It sickened him to think that this idiot might put a baby in danger to get to Elise.

Colt nodded, got to his feet. "I'll call Reed and have him meet us at your house, and one of the hands can follow us over there. Plus, the CSI team is still out there going through the barn rubble."

Maybe all that law enforcement around meant it was the last place Buddy or their attacker would show up. Ever. Because Colt was tired of Elise having to go through one nightmare after another.

"I can also have the Rangers meet us at your place so it cuts down on time you're out on the road," he added. "That way, they can take you straight from there to the safe house."

It took Colt a few minutes to make the arrangements

for what he hoped would be a short, safe trip, and then with Elise in tow, he went looking through the house for his father. He found him and Rosalie in the kitchen. His sister had a sleeping baby on her lap, so Colt made the goodbyes quiet and quick.

Elise certainly didn't object.

Despite the welcome that she'd gotten from Rosalie and Roy, it was clear she wasn't comfortable there.

Colt took Elise onto the porch, but he didn't move her to his truck until the ranch hand, Darnell Tate, had driven around the side of the house so he was in place to follow them.

"Stay low in the seat," Colt reminded her when they got in.

She did, but she kept her head just high enough so she could look around. The same thing Colt was doing. Even though Elise's place was only about fifteen minutes away, it would feel like a long drive.

Colt had barely made it off McKinnon land when his phone buzzed, and he saw Cooper's name on the caller ID.

"Did you find Buddy?" Colt asked his brother the moment he answered the call.

"Not yet. But one of those private investigators that Joplin hired did find something out at the creek near the Braddock cabin."

Colt certainly hadn't forgotten about the PIs, but he'd put that way on the back burner. "What?" he asked, but judging from his brother's hesitation, this was about to be yet another dose of bad news.

"A bone fragment," Cooper said. "It was only about twenty yards from the cabin."

Elise obviously heard that, and since she was trying to move closer to the phone, Colt put it on speaker.

"And?" Colt pressed when Cooper didn't continue.

"They're pretty sure it doesn't belong to an animal. It seems to be human."

Colt let that sink in a moment. "They think it belongs to Whitt Braddock?"

"Yeah. But it'll have to be tested, of course."

Of course. And if it did turn out to belong to Whitt, it was yet more proof of murder. Not that the prosecution needed more. There'd been enough blood found at the scene to indicate Whitt was dead, but without a body, there was always a question that somehow he'd managed to survive.

A bone fragment shot that question to Hades and back.

"Why did it take so long to find it?" Colt asked. "We've had CSIs out there, and the county sheriff's team went over it just a couple of months ago."

Heck, over the years he and his brothers had looked for anything that would prove their mother had murdered Whitt.

"It's a small piece," Cooper explained. "Easy to miss because of all the rocks."

Yeah, but the timing was suspicious for it to turn up now. Of course, maybe he felt that way because of all the other stuff happening. Colt couldn't see, though, how any of their suspects could use this to their advantage.

"I'll keep you posted," Cooper said, and he ended the call.

Colt dropped the phone on the seat between Elise and him, and in the process got a glimpse of her expression. "I'm sorry," she whispered.

So was he. And he groaned. "This could go against my dad."

She made a small sound of agreement. "Because a jury might think he helped Jewell move the body."

It wouldn't matter if Roy hadn't been the one to kill Whitt, but an accessory carried the same penalty as murder. Death.

"Has your mother ever talked about what happened that day?" Elise asked.

Colt automatically started to clam up. Something he usually did when anyone mentioned his mother and the murder. But Elise had just as much of a stake in this as he did. And his softened feelings toward her didn't help, either. Hard to play mute with someone he'd kissed like crazy.

"She's never talked to me about it," Colt answered. "And the only thing my dad has said was that he was drunk and doesn't remember much. Still, I think he'd remember dragging a body from the cabin to the creek."

Another sound of agreement. "And I certainly don't remember seeing anything like that." She paused. "What I do remember is that Whitt was a big man. So how does the DA think Jewell got his body out of the cabin?"

Colt lifted his shoulder. "There were drag marks leading out to where Whitt parked his truck when he used the cabin. People fueled with adrenaline can lift things they wouldn't be able to under normal circumstances."

But now there was a problem with that theory. If Jewell had managed somehow to get Whitt into the truck, then why hadn't she driven the body miles away? Why had she dumped him so close to the cabin that all these years later, a bone fragment would be found?

"Don't borrow trouble," Elise reminded him. "The bone isn't necessarily a game changer."

No, but Colt didn't like the fact that it could make this

situation turn even uglier for his father. Still, he couldn't see Joplin planting something like that, either, because it would still hurt Jewell in the long run.

His phone buzzed again. Not Cooper this time. Instead, he saw a message from the Texas Ranger on the screen.

Safe house is ready. On my way to Ms. Nichols's place now to pick her up.

He handed the phone to Elise so she could read it for herself. They'd both known this was coming, but it suddenly seemed as if it was happening way too fast for Colt. Judging from the way Elise pulled in her breath, it did to her, too.

"We'll find Buddy or whoever's behind this," Colt reminded her. "After that, you won't need a safe house."

Or him.

But that was a good thing, he reminded himself. Elise and he both needed to get on with their lives. And if they got together again for another kissing session, it sure as heck wouldn't be fueled by fear and adrenaline.

"You'll be at the sheriff's office for the hypnosis tomorrow?" she asked.

"Sure." However, Joplin might find some way to block him and his brothers from being with Elise during the actual session. Still, Joplin couldn't stop him from being in the building.

And then something occurred to him. Something bad.

"Do you think you could have blocked out...something more than what you saw?" he asked.

"I'm not sure." She answered so quickly that it was obvious she'd given it some thought. "I have wondered why it took me so long to remember seeing Roy. Twenty-three years," she mumbled. "I didn't remember any of it until I read about Jewell's arrest."

Yeah, and that bothered him, too. A lot. Not because he thought she was lying about the memory but because she could remember so much more. After all, people blocked out bad stuff all the time. Especially bad stuff.

"Why were you even by the creek that day?" Colt asked.

She glanced at him. "Because of you. Remember?"

No. He didn't.

Wait.

He did.

"You'd come to the ranch earlier with your grandmother. She was picking up a calf that she'd bought from Dad. I was talking to you, and my brothers started teasing me about liking you."

"And you got mad and said I was the last girl in Texas that you'd ever like," she finished for him.

Yes, he had said that, along with a few other not so nice things. "I'm sorry."

"You were nine years old," Elise reminded him. "Like killing spiders, being mean to girls came with the territory."

"But I clearly upset you. You went to the creek to blow off some steam?"

She smiled softly. "I went there to cry, and then I tried to think up some curse that I could put on you. Hey, I was nine, too," she added when he gave her a hard look. "I wanted a little payback."

Her smile vanished as quickly as it'd come. "But I didn't think payback would mean your family being torn apart."

He was about to tell her that she'd in no way been responsible for that. Nope, that was solely on his mother's shoulders because even if his father had been an accessory, Whitt wouldn't have died if Jewell hadn't gotten involved with him in the first place. However, before Colt could say anything, his phone buzzed again, and it was another call from his brother.

Maybe this time, it'd be good news.

"The CSI out at Elise's place just called," Cooper said.

"Please tell me they found prints to ID the person who rigged that booby trap," Colt grumbled.

"No. It's worse than that. They found a body."

Chapter Ten

Elise was back to pacing across the room again. This time it wasn't at the McKinnon ranch but in the kitchen of her own home. She was afraid to ask herself what else could go wrong because it was obvious that plenty could.

A body. On her land.

Yes, that was plenty bad.

She glanced out at the yellow crime-scene tape that now surrounded the very spot where she'd planned on building the new barn and stables. A fresh start for her return to Sweetwater Springs.

But it didn't feel so much like a fresh start now.

Along with Cooper, there was Reed and a trio of CSIs. All of them were focused on the small area where the forensic investigator was carefully digging. Both Cooper and Reed were on their phones, no doubt coordinating what would turn out to be yet another investigation—depending on what they were about to uncover.

And according to the CSIs, what they were about to uncover was a body.

"There's no need for you to watch that," Colt said to her.

He'd just finished his latest call—this one to tell the Ranger to delay picking her up for the safe house. Something that Elise had demanded that Colt do. She wasn't leaving until she'd learned whose body they were digging up.

He walked to her, gently taking hold of her arm and trying to urge her into the living room. But Elise stayed put.

"What if it's Whitt Braddock?" she said, repeating what had been going through her mind since she'd first heard the news. "What if my gran had some part in this? After all, she and Jewell were friends. She could have helped her."

"Don't," Colt insisted. "Remember when you told me not to borrow trouble? Well, now, I'm telling you the same thing. There's no immediate way of knowing how long that body's been out there. There are even some Indian burial grounds around here."

Elise wanted to believe that. Mercy, did she, but she kept going back to that bone fragment that'd just been found by the creek. Maybe Jewell had dumped the body and then moved it later.

But when would she have done that?

Colt's mother left town just days after Whitt's disappearance. Not much time to do something like this, and it didn't make sense that Jewell would move the body from the woods near the creek to a place on her gran's ranch where it could have been dug up at any time. Heck, it was only about twenty yards from the house, and in the very spot where her gran's rose garden had once been. Elise had played there too many times to count.

It sickened her to think that she might have been playing on top of a dead body that whole time.

"You're trembling," Colt pointed out. "And if you

don't come and sit down, I'll have to do something to distract you."

His gaze dropped to her mouth.

That surprised her. "Are you threatening me with a kiss?" she asked.

He lifted his shoulder. "Whatever works. The one thing that isn't going to work is you pacing and driving yourself nuts. Come on. Sit down."

His grip on her stayed gentle. Barely a touch. But it was enough to get her moving to the sofa. Part of her hated that Colt could so easily persuade her to do something, but she was thankful he was there.

Even if he'd used the kiss threat.

Something that wasn't actually a threat when she knew it would be a nice distraction that her body would appreciate.

Colt sat next to her, pulling her into the curve of his arm. All in all, a comforting place to be. Well, it was until her thoughts went back to what was going on just yards away.

"I wish they'd just hurry and dig it up," she mumbled. Not that it would help with the wild scenarios going through her head. Even if it didn't turn out to be Whitt, there was still someone's dead body out there.

"You can always wait at the safe house," he offered, "and I'll call you the second we know anything."

It wasn't the first time he'd made the offer, and Elise figured he'd continue to make it as long as she stayed put. And as long as she was as visibly shaken as she was now. "I haven't made up my mind if I want to go or not."

Colt didn't roll his eyes exactly, but it was close. "You can't possibly want to stay here."

"No. At least not until that body is gone. But I'm

not sure I want to go to a strange place with, well, a stranger."

Elise waited for him to try to convince her that the Ranger who would be guarding her wouldn't be a stranger for long. And that he would be someone she could trust. He didn't do either of those things. Colt only made a sound of agreement and pulled her deeper into his arms.

"We'll work it out," he said, brushing a kiss on her forehead.

And that's how his brother Cooper found them when he came in through the back door. Colt's mouth on her forehead. Her, snuggled in his arms. Colt and she immediately moved apart, but Cooper couldn't have missed the close contact between them.

Unlike Rosalie and Roy, there was no warm welcome from Cooper. In his divided family, Cooper was clearly on his father's side, and he saw her as a potential threat. Or maybe the look he was giving her was because he now saw her as someone connected to the body they'd just found.

Cooper was wearing his usual "uniform" of jeans, white shirt, a Stetson and boots, with his badge pinned to his belt beneath his buckskin jacket. His eyes and dark brown hair were a genetic copy of Colt's, and like Colt, Elise had no trouble seeing the fatigue and stress in his eyes.

"Anything yet?" Colt asked, getting to his feet. Elise did, too, and she tried to move away from Colt, but he held on, dropping his arm from her shoulders to her waist so he could anchor her in place.

"It'll be a while before the body's fully excavated. They're being careful because they don't want to disturb anything around it in case it might contain evidence.

But it's definitely not a Native American burial. There are clothing fragments on the remains. What appears to be denim."

So, it was someone wearing jeans. Someone like Whitt. That caused the knot in Elise's stomach to tighten even more.

"How did they even discover the body?' she asked. "Because I certainly didn't see any signs of it."

"The CSIs brought out a cadaver dog to go through the barn rubble. They wanted to make sure the person who set the trip wire hadn't been killed and buried in the process. The dog sensed something all right but not at the barn. The CSI dug around and found the body in a fairly shallow grave."

Just those two words, *shallow grave*, sent a cold shiver down her. "I swear I didn't know anything about this," she said to Cooper.

If he believed her, he made no indication whatsoever. Instead, his attention went to his brother. "I just got an update from the Appaloosa Pass deputy handling the roadblock. Still no sign of Buddy."

Great. The man had nine lives when it came to escaping, and until they caught him, Cooper or Colt couldn't question him about his involvement in all of this. However, no matter what Buddy said, he was still her top suspect for what'd happened in that barn.

"But there is some good news," Cooper went on. "The county DA isn't arresting Dad for these attacks. Not yet, anyway. And Joplin's request for a mistrial was denied."

It was indeed good news, even though that meant she'd be testifying, after all. She wasn't looking forward to that, but Elise was glad that Joplin hadn't managed to put a stop to the trial before it'd even started.

Colt and his family needed closure. Heck, so did she. Though she wasn't sure how any of them would feel if *closure* landed their father in jail.

"I'm sorry if all of this put your family in danger," Elise said.

Something flashed through Cooper's eyes. Anger, no doubt. But then those hard eyes softened a bit, and he scrubbed his hand over his face. "What time is she seeing the hypnotist tomorrow?" he asked Colt.

"Eight in the morning."

Cooper nodded. "Stay with her until then. I'm putting you back on protection detail."

The relief flooded through her. Too much relief, considering that she figured Colt might be ready to put some distance between them. But then she saw the quick glance that the brothers shared and knew there was more to this.

"What happened?" Colt asked.

Cooper pulled in a long breath, nodded. "The woman Elise investigated, Meredith Darrow, is making waves. She's filing a lawsuit against Elise for defamation of character, but I'm not as concerned about her as I am about her brother, Leo."

"Her brother?" Elise and Colt repeated in unison. "Why would he have any part in this?" Elise added.

"Because he's a small-time thug, that's why, and he came by the sheriff's office demanding to see you. I won't repeat the names he called you," Cooper said to Elise. "He didn't exactly threaten you, but it was close."

Oh, mercy. She so didn't need this on top of everything else. Colt's arm went back around her.

"Did you arrest him?" Colt asked, and judging from his tone, he was just as riled about this as she was upset.

Cooper shook his head. "No cause. *Yet.* But I did

issue him a few threats of my own and gave him a ticket for illegally parking outside the office. That didn't help his temper," Cooper added. "I checked, and Leo has a record for assault and a couple of restraining orders against him from former girlfriends and employers. He's obviously very protective of his sister, so he might cause some trouble. You'll need to be on the lookout for him, along with getting your own restraining order if he doesn't back off."

Great. Now, in addition to a dead body and the idiot trying to kill them, they also had to worry about a hothead.

Except they might be one and the same.

"Leo could be behind the attacks," Elise concluded, and neither Colt nor Cooper disagreed with her. Any man who'd used violence in the past was probably inclined to use it again.

"We'll be tied up here for a while yet," Cooper went on a moment later, "but the sheriff in Appaloosa Pass said he'd bring in Leo and question him for us. I figure it'll just rile Leo even more, but maybe he'll do something stupid like take a swing at the sheriff, so they can arrest him and get him off the streets."

It was a testament to how crazy her life was that she actually hoped Leo did try to assault a lawman. They already had enough suspects out there without adding another one to the mix. Especially one who felt he had to avenge his sister and her illegal activity.

"There's more," Cooper went on, and she could tell from his expression that this was more bad news. "I just talked to the Rangers before I came in, and someone's trying to follow the sergeant who was coming out here to pick up Elise."

Yes, definitely bad. It meant someone had likely

learned that she was to be taken to a safe house. If their attacker discovered the location, it would make her an easy target. Again.

"The Ranger will try to get an ID on the person following him, but it's probably best if Elise stays put for a while. When I can, I'll escort you to the sheriff's office. You can stay there until we make sure it's safe to head to the new location."

Elise was afraid that might never happen. Hard to feel safe with her world crashing down around her.

"It's not much," Cooper went on, "but there's a small flop room just off the break area at the sheriff's office. It has a single bed and bathroom. It won't be comfortable, but it might work out better if you stayed there tonight so someone can help Colt guard you."

"Yes," she immediately agreed.

She was a trouble magnet these days, and with someone trying to follow the Ranger, the sheriff's office was better than going back to the McKinnon ranch where Colt's family could be hurt. Plus, Colt would have backup at the sheriff's office and maybe their attacker would be less likely to come after her there.

Maybe.

Cooper turned to leave but then stopped. "I'm sorry," he added as he walked out.

Coming from him that was practically a hug, but it was Colt who actually did it. He wrapped his arms around her and pulled her close.

"I'm sorry," Colt repeated.

That helped, too, but Elise felt if she stayed still, she might explode.

"I have to do something. *Anything.*" She glanced around at her already clean kitchen. For once she wasn't pleased about being a neat person.

"You should pack some things before we leave," Colt suggested.

Yes, and it would get her moving. Better than pacing and waiting by the window for them to pull the body out of the ground. Elise headed toward her bedroom.

Colt followed her, of course. With everything going on, he probably wasn't going to let her out of his sight— something she didn't mind.

Elise took an overnight bag from the shelf in her closet and stuffed it with a pair of jeans. She managed to pack some sweaters before the first tear spilled down her cheek.

Mercy, she was a wreck.

Colt made a soft sigh, and before the second tear came, he already had her in his arms again. Something he'd been doing way too much of lately, but like the other times, Elise didn't resist. However, she did try to stave off a full-fledged crying jag.

She failed at that, too.

"I hate crying," she mumbled.

"Seems to me that you've got a solid reason to cry. If it helps, I can lend you a shoulder or two."

"Your shoulders always help," she answered, her voice a choked whisper. "That's part of the problem." Elise pulled back, and even though she figured she looked pretty bad with her red eyes and puffy face, she still met his gaze. "What are we doing, Colt?"

Thankfully, she didn't have to explain that. She could see that he knew what she meant, and he sighed again. "To hell if I know. Seems as if we picked up where we left off as kids."

They had, but the situation wasn't nearly the same as it was back then. "Your brothers—"

But that was all she managed to get out before he

kissed her again. It was instantly one of those mind-numbing ones, and he was so good at it. Too good. It dried up her tears, fast, but it replaced her feeling of doom and gloom with more of that heat that she knew would only complicate things.

Still, that didn't stop her. Elise melted into the kiss, and let Colt's clever mouth ease her fears. Okay, it did more than ease them. That coil of heat went a long way to getting her mind on other things. Like more kissing.

More everything.

Colt and she had never gotten past the make-out stage, but her imagination was pretty good in that area. If this was how she felt just kissing him, then landing in bed would be an experience to remember.

Elise held on to that. Held on to him, too. And let his mouth work some magic on the rest of her body.

For a few seconds, anyway.

She pulled back even though that was the last thing she wanted to do. What she wanted was to test that landing-in-bed theory. Especially since the bed was just a few feet away.

Colt glanced at the bed. Then, at her. So not good. Because they were both thinking the very thing that could get them in trouble.

Thank goodness the only thing that saved them was that there was a team of lawmen just outside the window and any one of them could come walking in at any minute. Cooper had already caught them in a semi-intimate embrace. Best not to let him walk in on something that Colt and she shouldn't even be thinking about doing.

"I would say that won't happen again," Colt mumbled. "But I don't like lying to myself."

That made her smile, and Elise realized Colt was

probably the only person on earth who could make her do that right now. And that was a huge red flag.

Because she was falling hard for him.

Another *so not good*. It meant she was fast on her way to a broken heart, and Elise wasn't sure she was mentally strong enough to deal with that right now.

That didn't mean she couldn't put off a broken heart until later, though.

She heard the sound of the door opening in another part of the house. Colt moved ahead of her, and they hurried back into the kitchen just as Cooper was walking in.

"It's not Whitt," Cooper immediately said.

Elise released the breath that she'd just sucked in. Yes, there was still a body buried on her property, but at least her gran hadn't had anything to do with Whitt's murder.

"Any idea who it is?" Colt asked his brother.

"It's a woman by the name of Brandy Seaver, from San Antonio. Her wallet was in her jeans, and the driver's license matches the description of the body. Did you know her?" Cooper asked Elise.

She repeated the name, trying to figure out if it rang any bells. It didn't. So, Elise shook her head. "Who is she?"

"I made a quick call after we found the wallet and ID," Cooper went on. "Brandy Seaver had a long record of prostitution, mainly in San Antonio, and a missing person's report was filed on her nearly a year ago."

A year ago. When Elise had still been living in Dallas. She hated to think of something like that now, but at least it meant Cooper might believe she didn't have anything to do with putting the woman's body in the ground.

"How did this Brandy Seaver get out here to Sweetwater Springs?" Colt asked his brother.

"According to the report that SAPD just sent me, the girls who worked the streets with Brandy said she was last seen getting into a truck with a *customer*. None of them got the license-plate number, but several were able to describe the vehicle and the driver."

Cooper paused. "The description of the driver matches Buddy to a tee."

Chapter Eleven

Colt rolled over, the pain shooting through his shoulder and back, and he groaned out loud before he could stop himself. The groan immediately grabbed Elise's attention because she jackknifed to a sitting position. Her breath already gusting. Her eyes wide with concern.

And she looked down at him from the small twin bed. It was really more like a glorified cot in the break room at the sheriff's office.

"You're in pain," she said.

"Just not used to sleeping on the floor," Colt assured her. And a hard tile floor at that.

He worked his way out of the sleeping bag and would have gotten to his feet. If his feet hadn't both been asleep, that is. He had no choice but to drop onto the bed next to her.

The very place he'd been trying hard to avoid for the past eight hours.

Now, here he was. In bed, literally, with Elise. And despite the lack of sleep and mussed hair, she managed to look way past the hot stage. Of course, she always managed to look hot, so that was nothing new.

"I'm moving," he insisted.

But she took hold of his arm and scooted over so that she was pressed right against the wall. "We can control ourselves for at least a minute or two while you get the feeling back in your feet."

Colt tried to smile, failed. Because being this close to her was a special form of torture. "After the dream I had about you, I shouldn't be within a mile of you," he mumbled.

"I hope it was sexual." Her eyes widened again when he looked at her. "I mean better sexual than your wanting to wring my neck."

He leaned in, risked brushing a kiss on her cheek. "There are a lot of things I want to do to you, but wringing your neck's not on the list. Kissing it sounds like a good way to start the morning, though."

And a bad one, too. Because he hadn't been kidding about that dream. It had been a scorcher. Him and Elise butt naked, not on some tiny bed or floor, either. His bed. And they'd done things that he'd been thinking about doing with her for days.

Like kissing her.

Tasting every inch of her.

Sinking hard and deep into her.

Then, kissing her again.

So, that's exactly what he did. He kissed her, knowing that it was a dumber-than-dirt kind of thing to do. Despite the pain and numb feet, every other part of him was humming and aching for her.

"Bad idea?" she questioned, his mouth hovering over hers.

"Oh, yeah. The worst idea."

Somehow, that made the kiss even better. He'd never been into the whole forbidden-fruit fantasy, but in Elise's case, he'd make an exception. So, he upped the *worst idea* into a full-blown kiss. But he didn't go after her mouth this time. He went after her neck again so he could finish what he'd started.

Well, finish a little part of it, anyway.

He could do something about tasting her.

Oh, man. She was just as good as he'd imagined she would be.

Colt enjoyed the little shivering sound that Elise made when his mouth touched her throat. Enjoyed even more the kick he felt in his own body. The taste of her cruised right through him—all fire and heat—and one part of him in particular was urging him to go in for more.

Which would definitely lead to down-and-dirty morning sex.

Really not a good idea since they were just one wall away from the squad room where Cooper, Reed and heaven knew who else was already at work.

That didn't make pulling away from her easier, though, and Colt couldn't quite stop himself. He added yet another kiss several inches lower and heard another of those silky sounds of need from her.

Yet more fire and heat.

Too much for just kisses.

She eased back, her gaze connecting with his. Uh-oh. There wasn't a let's-stop-this-now kind of look in her eyes. It was pure need. And plenty of it. Probably the same amount mirrored in his, and Colt figured if he kissed her again, he was going to forget all about that one-wall barrier and go for broke.

And he'd regret it.

Maybe not while he was deep inside her. But later. The last thing Elise needed was a sex-clouded mind. Ditto for him. If he had any chance of protecting her, then he had to stay out of her bed.

Easier said than done. But Colt forced his mind back on what it should have been on in the first place.

He checked his watch. Cleared his throat. He didn't dare try to stand yet and seriously doubted he could walk.

"The hypnotist will be here soon." he reminded her. "Why don't you go ahead and grab a shower."

They'd both taken one when they'd gotten in around 10:00 p.m., but at least a shower would get them off the bed.

Maybe.

"You want me to shower alone?" she asked.

Colt groaned. That didn't help. "No, I'd rather be in there with you and your soap-slick body, but that would fall into the worst-idea category. Best if you shower alone."

His body protested that, of course.

Elise leaned in, kissed him. That didn't help, either. Then she groaned.

"The shower," she repeated, and he didn't think it was his imagination that she had to force herself to leave. Colt sure had to force himself to let her leave.

Once she was in the shower with the water running, Colt groaned again. What he should do was stick his head, and another part of him, in a bucket of ice water to cool him down and maybe regain his senses. He was playing with fire when it came to Elise, and he was pretty sure both of them would end up getting burned.

Or worse.

If he didn't keep his focus, the danger was going to come back to bite him in the butt, and in this case it could get her killed. That reminder helped even more than a bucket of cold water.

His phone buzzed, and Colt rifled through the sleeping bag to find it. He figured it was Cooper, calling to make sure it was okay to come to the flop room, but it wasn't a number that Colt recognized.

"It's me," the man said when Colt answered, and unlike the number, it was a voice he instantly recognized.

"Buddy," Colt *greeted*. "Where the hell are you?"

"Nowhere near you, so don't bother looking for me. Don't bother trying to trace this call, either, because I'm using one of those prepaid cell phones. I wanna talk to Elise now."

"She's busy." And Colt had no plans to unbusy her so she could take this call. "You can talk to me and not just over the phone. I want you down at the sheriff's office ASAP so we can chat face-to-face."

"Yeah, I'll bet you do so you can arrest me on the spot. Don't you think I know what in Sam Hill is going on? It's all over the news about the body that the cops dug up at Elise's place."

It didn't surprise Colt that the story had already made the news. Something like that couldn't be kept under wraps for long, especially since there was an APB out for Buddy's arrest.

"You need to turn yourself in," Colt insisted.

"Not gonna happen. I didn't kill that woman."

"But she got in the truck with you on the very night that she disappeared." Colt had read all the details in the report that SAPD had sent Cooper. "That makes you a prime suspect."

Buddy didn't jump to deny that, but he did hesitate. "Yeah, she was with me. So what? Doesn't mean nothing."

"Did you kill her?" Colt came right out and asked.

Again, Buddy hesitated. "No. She started whining about wanting more money for staying the whole night.

We got in an argument, I maybe sort of pushed her to stop her from slapping me, and she fell and hit her head on the kitchen counter. I didn't kill her."

It would be days or even weeks before a cause of death could be determined, but a fatal blow to the head should show some kind of trauma. Of course, it might not tell if it was accidental or intentional.

"If that's really what happened, then why didn't you just call Cooper and tell him there'd been an accident?" Colt pressed.

"Because I figured he wouldn't believe me, that's why." Buddy no longer sounded hesitant, and he cursed. "I also figured nobody would miss her. She was just a working girl. Lower than dirt. I probably gave her a better burial than she would have gotten on the street."

Even though Colt didn't know the dead woman, it turned his stomach to hear Buddy talk about her that way. Once he caught up with Buddy, he'd do whatever it took to make the man pay. Because even if this had been an accident—and Colt doubted that it was—the woman still deserved a whole lot better than being buried in a shallow grave.

"All of this is Elise's fault," Buddy continued at the exact moment that Elise came out of the bathroom.

She mouthed, "Who is it?"

Colt wasn't especially eager for her to hear what this dirtbag was saying, but he couldn't keep it from her, either. However, he did motion for her to keep quiet. No way did he want her in a shouting match with Buddy, and that's what would happen if she heard Buddy blaming her for everything.

"If Elise had just sold me the place like I wanted," Buddy went on, "then nobody would have ever found that girl."

"And you would have gotten away with murder," Colt promptly reminded him.

"I told you that it wasn't murder!" Buddy shouted. "It was an accident, and if I'd thought you and your brother would have given me a fair shake, I would have already told you about it."

The color drained from Elise's face. She likely already knew that Buddy had killed the woman, but it clearly hit her hard to hear it spelled out like that.

"So instead you decided to try to run Elise off her own land," Colt said. "When trashing the place, intimidation and graffiti didn't work, then you escalated things by rigging the barn so that it'd fall and kill us."

"What?" Buddy asked, sounding surprised.

Of course, the man could be faking that particular emotion. Murdering the prostitute wasn't personal, but an attack against Elise and him certainly was. Buddy had to know something like that would make Colt come after him and come after him hard.

"You heard me," Colt snapped. "You tried to kill us."

"I didn't." And Buddy repeated it several times. Not a shout, either, like before. He was mumbling like a confused man. Or a man pretending to be confused. "That barn was old. It probably just fell on its own."

"No. It had some help, and I don't think it's a coincidence that it happened shortly after you went to the barn and got that box. Did you set the booby trap then, or did you wait until nightfall?"

Buddy cursed. "I knew calling you was a mistake. Tell Elise what I said." And with that, he hung up.

Elise stood there, waiting for him to fill her in, but Colt took a deep breath first. "Buddy's blaming everyone but himself for the dead body. He said it was an accident, that the woman fell and hit her head."

"You believe him?"

"No." But Colt immediately had to rethink that. "Maybe, about that part, anyway."

Elise stayed quiet a moment, obviously giving it some thought, too, and she made a sound of agreement. "But if Buddy owned up to the woman's death and the vandalism, why wouldn't he also just admit he rigged the barn?"

Colt shrugged. "Maybe because he knew it'd make me come after him." However, Buddy had to know that Colt was already after him. "But if that's not the reason, I'll find out as soon as I talk to him."

That meant keeping the pressure on to find Buddy, and while a burner cell phone couldn't be traced, they might be able to locate the tower that'd been used for the call. If so, they could get a general idea of Buddy's location and find out if the man was still near Sweetwater Springs.

He made a quick call to Reed to tell him about the call so the deputy could get started on the trace. Colt would also need to write down everything the man said in case it was later needed for a trial. And unless Buddy made some kind of plea deal, it would be needed.

"Give me a minute to wash up," Colt told Elise. "And then I'll get to work so we can find some answers to all these questions."

Colt hurried because he was anxious to get started but also because Elise didn't look too steady on her feet. That caused him to curse. She wasn't getting many moments of peace and quiet these days, and Buddy's call certainly hadn't helped.

She was sitting at the foot of the bed, staring down at her hands when he came back into the room. "Don't let Buddy get to you," he said, but he already knew that the man had managed to do just that. "Now that he's confessed to burying the woman, we can arrest him. And it won't be hard to pin murder charges on him."

Elise nodded. "But I still have to get past the hypnosis."

He certainly hadn't forgotten that some big bad memories could be uncovered during that session.

"One step at a time," he reminded her. Reminded himself, too. "I'll call the diner and have them send over some breakfast."

But when Colt led her into the squad room, he saw that someone had already taken care of that. There were pastries and coffee—thank God. He poured a cup for each of them, but after seeing Cooper's expression, Colt wished he had a shot of something a little stronger.

"You weren't able to get the tower for Buddy's call," Colt concluded.

"Nothing on that yet," Cooper answered. "But I just got word Frank Wellerman's going to turn Elise's report over to SAPD so they can question Meredith about possible embezzlement activity at her last job. Let's just say Meredith's not too happy about that. She's called here twice already looking for Elise."

Colt definitely didn't like the sound of that. "Any chance Meredith will go out to our ranch looking for her?"

"Maybe. I've already alerted Dad and the ranch hands. We're locking down the place for a while."

"Oh, God," Elise mumbled. "I'm so sorry."

"No need to be," Cooper assured her. "This is on her, not you. In fact, none of this is on you. I've got Reed looking into both Meredith and her brother. Maybe something else will pop up that we can use to file our own charges against them."

Cooper's attention turned back to Colt. "Here's the second round of news that you probably don't want to hear before having coffee. Since Joplin's request for a mistrial was denied, he's trying a different angle. He's trying to have Elise declared a hostile witness so he can have her removed from our protective custody."

Colt should have seen this coming, but then he hadn't exactly had a lot of time to sit down and try to figure out what Joplin might do next. Obviously, the lawyer was doing everything he could to get Elise away from the McKinnons.

"Will Joplin succeed?" Elise asked, the worry dripping from her voice.

Cooper lifted his shoulder. "Joplin's claiming that you two are having an affair and that Colt is exerting undue influence over you that could in turn affect your testimony."

Hell. After all the dirty thoughts he'd had about Elise, it probably did look as if they were sleeping together, and Joplin had arrived at the ranch shortly after Elise and he had had a steamy kissing session.

Now it was Elise who cursed. "I'm sick and tired of that man. It's none of his business if Colt and I are having an affair. And since when would sex—even great sex—fry my brain to the point where I couldn't tell the truth under oath during a murder trial?"

She glanced around at Cooper, him and the other two deputies in the room. "Sorry," she mumbled, obviously a little embarrassed about that great-sex comment. But then the embarrassment faded, and she snapped back toward Cooper. "Can I get a restraining order against Joplin because this is harassment?"

Cooper didn't actually smile, but it was close. "I'll see what I can do." Thankfully, his brother didn't touch that great-sex comment, didn't address a possible affair between them, either, and he strolled in the direction of his office.

"No need to say you're sorry again," Colt said when Elise opened her mouth. And since she immediately closed it, he figured he'd pegged exactly what she'd been about to say to him. "Cooper's right. This isn't your fault."

She shook her head. "But it certainly feels that way."

Even though they weren't alone, Colt put his coffee aside and pulled her to him. "Try to eat something," he coaxed. "The hypnotist will be here soon. Since the session might take a while, you don't want to start it on an empty stomach."

However, the words had no sooner left his mouth when a car pulled into the parking lot of the sheriff's office. Elise probably wasn't mentally ready for the appointment. Colt wasn't sure he was, either. But whatever she might remember was just something they'd have to face.

Like all the other junk that'd been coming their way.

"Oh, no," Elise mumbled, her attention on the side window that faced the parking lot. "Not this. Not now."

Colt immediately saw what had caused that reaction, and while it was already too late to block the door, he did step in front of Elise in case this turned as ugly as he was afraid it might.

The door flew open.

Meredith tried to come in, but the hulk of a man next to her practically shoved her aside, and he stormed into the building first. Even though Colt had never met the man, he recognized him from the photo that'd come up during the background check.

Leo Darrow.

"Where the hell is Elise Nichols?" Leo snarled. "Because it's payback time for what she's trying to do to my sister."

Chapter Twelve

Elise hated having yet another confrontation, especially since the morning had already started out with that phone call from Buddy. But there was no way she would back down from this despite the fact that Leo was downright intimidating.

Ignoring Colt's warning for her to stay put, Elise stepped to his side and faced Leo and Meredith head-on. It was actually a good thing that her stitches were throbbing and that she hadn't dosed up with caffeine yet because that would help her give the pair as ornery a look as they were giving her.

Leo certainly looked menacing with his heavily muscled body and flattened nose. A sign that it'd been broken a few times—no doubt in bar fights. There were nicks and scars on his face, and along with the bulging veins on his neck, Elise figured his idea of *payback* was physical violence. Something he looked more than capable of doing.

Reed obviously thought so, too, because even though he was on the phone, he stood, moving closer to Colt and her. Still, Elise figured two armed lawmen weren't going to stop Leo and Meredith from speaking their piece.

Hopefully, speaking was all they would do.

Of course, if they did something violent, or just plain

stupid, then it would give Colt a reason to arrest them on the spot.

"Frank Wellerman's turning over your report to the cops," Meredith said, stepping to her brother's side, too.

Elise nodded. "I heard."

Meredith had to get her jaw unclenched before she could speak again. "The cops will think I did something wrong."

Good. Because she had. "Trust me, as bad as your day's been, I've got you beat. And if you're here to demand I pull the report that I wrote up on you, then you're wasting your time."

"Oh, you're pulling that report, all right," Leo insisted, and the step he took toward her had Colt taking a step of his own. Colt also put his hand over the gun in his holster.

"You'll want to take a moment," Colt warned him. "So you think about what you might or might not do in the next couple of seconds. If you're wanting to spend a lot of time in jail, then go ahead and come closer."

Leo stopped, all right. Well, he stopped moving, anyway, but the venomous look he aimed at Elise only got worse.

"If the cops believe your lies, my sister could go to jail," he said as if that excused his behavior.

"That's not my call," Elise answered. "I only reported the facts as I found them. I didn't tell Mr. Wellerman what to do with the information I gave him."

"Facts," Leo spat out. "Yeah, right. If you get your way, you'll have the cops looking at both of us for something we didn't do."

"If you're innocent, you'll be able to prove that in a court of law, won't you?" Colt argued. "But coming here like this darn sure won't help your case."

"To hell it won't," Leo argued right back. Except he turned to Elise. "You don't think I have friends? I can ruin any chance you have of continuing this line of so-called work you do."

"I'm sure you have friends," she answered before Colt could issue another threat. "I have them, too, and if I want to keep working, then I will."

"We'll see about that," Meredith snapped. "I'm going through with my defamation of character lawsuit, and—"

"Hold that thought," Reed interrupted, and while he finished his phone call, he lifted his index finger in a wait-a-section gesture. The moment he hung up, the deputy handed the notes that he'd been taking to Colt.

"What now?" Meredith snapped. "More lies and allegations about me?"

Elise didn't get a chance to read the note before Colt dropped it on his desk and shot a glare at Leo.

"Tell me about Simon Martinelli," Colt ordered, and there was no mistaking his tone. It was an order.

Meredith shook her head, maybe pretending not to recognize the name. But Elise certainly did. It was the now-dead hit man who'd run her off the road.

"What about him?" Leo countered. "He has nothing to do with this."

Colt shook his head. "Wrong answer, try again. You knew Martinelli."

Oh, mercy. This wasn't a connection she wanted. A thug paired with a hit man. And the timing of the attack could have meant that Leo had been the one to hire Martinelli.

Of course, Meredith could have done the hiring, too. And that meant this only complicated their investigation even more since Buddy, too, had known Martinelli, and Buddy had just as much motive as these two to hire a hit man.

"So?" Leo's chin came up a notch.

"So," Colt repeated. "Martinelli's dead."

Leo didn't seem the least bit surprised about that. Of course, it had been on the news, so he could have already heard. "I had nothing to do with that."

Elise had expected the denial. She certainly hadn't believed that Leo would confess to murder right here, right now. Though it would have made her life a whole lot easier, and safer, if he had.

"How about hiring Martinelli to come after Elise?" Colt countered. "Did you have something to do with that?"

"No!" he shouted at the same moment Meredith answered, "You're not dragging my brother into this. He's innocent, just trying to help me."

Elise doubted Leo was *innocent*, but she also doubted that just knowing a hit man was enough to arrest Leo.

Maybe Leo would throw a punch or something, after all.

"Call and put a freeze on their bank records," Colt told Reed, and the deputy immediately took out his phone to do that. "I want to see if either of these clowns have some suspicious payouts that could have gone to Martinelli."

"You can't do that," Meredith insisted.

"Let 'em," Leo disagreed. "They won't find anything."

Meredith made a sound of outrage that caused her mouth to tremble. "I've already had my privacy violated enough. Come on," she said, taking hold of her brother's arm.

Leo obviously didn't want to budge, but Meredith got

him moving. "This isn't over," Meredith warned them, and she hurried out the door with Leo in tow.

"Good catch," Colt told Reed the moment that the pair was out of earshot. "How'd you find the connection between Leo and Martinelli?"

Reed lifted his shoulder. "I didn't. It was a bluff. I figured a thug like him would probably know another thug."

It was a bluff that'd worked since Leo had indeed admitted an association with the hit man.

"Thanks," Colt told him, and he kept his attention pinned to Meredith and Leo, watching them drive away before he turned back to Elise. "After your appointment, I'll see what I can do about getting you out of here. I figure sooner or later Joplin will want to pay you a visit."

He would. "You're talking about taking me to the safe house with the Ranger?" she asked.

"You could use my place instead," Reed quickly offered. "It's not that far out of town, it has a security system with all the doors and windows wired. Plus, I have two dogs who bark at everything. You're welcome to it since I'll be pulling duty here tonight. I can even call a couple of your ranch hands if you like and have them stay over just to keep watch."

Elise liked that idea much better than being taken miles and miles away.

Colt made a sound of agreement. "Thanks. Call the Rangers and cancel the plans for a safe house."

He'd hardly finished telling Reed that, however, when he snapped toward the window, and she saw yet someone else making their way toward the sheriff's office. It was a short woman with auburn hair, and she was carrying a bulky briefcase.

"I'm Suzanne Dawkins," their visitor said the moment she stepped inside the building. Her attention went straight to Elise. "I'm here for your hypnosis appointment."

Elise had known this was about to happen. But she still dreaded it. "I'm ready." A lie, but then she was as ready as she'd ever be. "Would it be okay, though, if Colt stayed with me during the session?"

Suzanne nodded, sighed and glanced around, looking as uncomfortable as Elise felt. "I need to tell you up front, though, that if you recall anything during the session, I can't swear it'll stay between us. I'm not your physician or a psychiatrist, so it's possible I can be subpoenaed to testify about what you recall."

And Joplin would definitely do that if it helped clear Jewell's name.

"You'll probably remember everything you say while under hypnosis. That includes any bad things you might have witnessed. It could mean dealing with some, well, disturbing images. So, you still want to go through with it?" Suzanne asked.

Elise looked at Colt, and he finally nodded. Elise nodded, too, though she hoped this didn't turn out to be a mistake.

One that could send Colt's father straight to jail for murder.

COLT STOOD NEAR the door of the flop room and waited for the hypnotist to continue questioning Elise.

He was saying a few prayers, too.

Prayers for his father, and for what could be a whole boatload of nightmarish memories that Elise might have to relive.

He hated that she had go to through this.

Suzanne had already given Elise some kind of meds,

and her eyelids were drooping while she drifted in and out of consciousness. Something that the hypnotist had explained would happen. She'd also been adamant that Colt not say a word because it could interfere with whatever Elise might say.

"Elise, you're back by the creek next to the Braddock cabin," Suzanne said, her voice a soothing whisper. "You're nine years old. Remember?"

"Yes," Elise mumbled. "I'm mad at Colt."

Despite everything, he smiled. Then he frowned. He'd been a nine-year-old butthead to upset her like that.

"But Colt's not with you at the creek, now, is he?" Suzanne went on. "Are you alone?"

Elise nodded. "I'm stirring the water with a stick."

Maybe trying to put that curse on him she'd mentioned.

"Did you go near the cabin or look in the window before you went to the creek?" she asked.

"I'm not allowed to go near the cabin. Gran's rules. Mr. Braddock doesn't like kids playing around it. Even his own kids. They aren't allowed to go there."

"Okay," Suzanne answered. "Do you hear anything or see anyone while you're stirring the water with the stick?"

"No." But then Elise paused. "Yeah. I hear a door closing, I think, and someone walking. He's walking up from behind the cabin." Another pause. "It's Colt's dad. Hi, Mr. Roy." Elise's voice was small now, and she was no doubt deep into that childhood memory.

"Did Mr. Roy answer you?" Suzanne asked.

Another head shake. "He stumbled on the porch step of the cabin and said some bad words that I can't repeat. Gran'll wash my mouth out with soap if I do."

Colt pulled in his breath, praying it was his father's stumbling and nothing else that'd caused the profanity.

"Elise," Suzanne said, "don't repeat the bad words, but I need you to look at Mr. Roy. Did he actually come out of the cabin?"

"Maybe. I heard a door close."

"But you're not sure that Mr. Roy was the one who closed it?" Suzanne asked the very question that Colt wanted her to ask.

"No. Not sure."

Good. Yeah, it was only a little doubt, but it was far better than Elise having seen his father come out of the cabin.

"Is it windy?" Suzanne continued.

Even though her eyes were closed, he could see them moving behind her eyelids. "Yes. The leaves are rattling on the trees." She paused. "I guess the wind coulda blown the door shut."

Colt added another *good*. Of course, that didn't clear his father. From what Elise was recalling, the door had been open and that meant someone had opened it.

"Is Mr. Roy alone, and what's he wearing?" the therapist asked.

Elise's forehead bunched up, the expression a person would make when concentrating. "Nobody's with him. And he's got on jeans, boots, a brown shirt and his hat."

"You're sure he's alone?"

"I'm sure," Elise said after several moments. "I don't see or hear anybody else. If somebody was inside, I'd think they'd hear Mr. McKinnon cussing and come out. He's not being very quiet 'cause he's banging his fist on the front door right now."

That put a too-clear picture in Colt's mind of what his dad was going through. Drunk and furious that his wife was having an affair with a man he considered his enemy. His father had gone to the cabin no doubt to confront them.

But Jewell and Whitt hadn't been there.

Well, Whitt hadn't been there alive, anyway. It was possible while all of this was going on that Whitt's body was inside and that his mother was hiding.

"Mr. Roy's still banging on the door," Elise continued several moments later. "And he's yelling for Mr. Braddock and Miss Jewell to open up. But I don't think anybody's in there. The place was quiet before Mr. Roy got there. If I'd seen Mr. Braddock, I wouldn't have hung around the creek. Gran's rules."

It was a good rule, too. Whitt wasn't a friendly sort, and Colt had been on the receiving end of some of Whitt's yelling when he'd caught him playing too close to the cabin. Of course, in hindsight, Whitt might have done that because he'd been trying to conceal the fact that he had Jewell in there with him. Since his mother had stayed quiet about the subject, Colt had no idea how long the affair had been going on.

"Is there anything odd about Mr. Roy's clothes?" Suzanne pressed when Elise didn't continue. "Is there maybe mud…or something else on them?"

That question required Colt to hold his breath again, and it didn't help that it seemed to take Elise an eternity to answer. "No mud, but his hair's messed up bad, and he's stumbling again. Cussing, too. I think he's had too much to drink."

Yeah, he had. Drunk, which left a lot of gaps in his memory. Gaps that Elise could be about to fill.

"You're sure about the mud?" Suzanne asked. "Take a closer look. Is there anything on Mr. McKinnon's clothes, anything wet maybe?"

Again, Elise took her time thinking about that. "No." She paused. "But he's got something in his hand."

Oh, man. Not a knife or a gun. If so, it would put his father at the murder scene with a potential murder weapon.

"What's in Mr. Roy's hand?" Suzanne asked.

Yet another pause. Even longer than the others. "A bottle. Of whiskey, I think. He keeps drinking from it in between all the yelling."

Colt tried to make his breath of relief as silent as possible.

"That's good, Elise," Suzanne said, sounding a little relieved, too. "Is there anything else you notice about Mr. Roy or the cabin? Think hard."

"Nothing else," she said after several moments. "I have to go home now. Can I leave?"

"Of course. Elise, I'm going to count to three, and when I reach three, you'll open your eyes, and you'll be back in the Sweetwater Springs Sheriff's Office." Suzanne counted off the numbers, and just as she'd said, when she reached three, Elise opened her eyes.

Despite the obvious fatigue, Elise's gaze went straight to Colt. "I remember everything I saw. No blood," she mumbled. "Your father's innocent."

Colt was glad she remembered what she'd told them. Glad of the outcome, too.

Of course, this was just the beginning, and while it cleared his father, it didn't mean the danger was over for Elise. Just the opposite. Buddy was still missing, and it was obvious that Joplin, Meredith and her idiot brother, Leo, had the potential to cause plenty of trouble.

"Elise might be a little drowsy for a while," Suzanne said, standing and gathering up her things. "And someone should stay with her just in case she has any adverse reactions to the mild sedative that I gave her."

"I'm not leaving her," Colt assured her.

The moment Suzanne left, Elise sat up, touching her fingers to her head.

"Are you in pain?" Colt immediately asked.

"No." She took several deep breaths. "In fact, I feel better than I have in the past couple of days." And to prove it, she got to her feet.

Colt was right there to catch her, but she didn't so much as wobble. "Did Joplin or Meredith come back while I was under?"

He shook his head.

"But they will," she added. "What are the odds that we can get out of here before then? Maybe go to Reed's house? I don't think i'm up to another battle today."

Colt wasn't at all sure about moving Elise, especially so soon after Suzanne had given her that mild sedative, but he wasn't up to doing battle, either. With his arm looped around her, they went back into the squad room, ready to ask Reed for the keys to his place, but the deputy was already one step ahead of him. He handed Colt a key and a piece of paper with the code for the security system.

"Stay as long as you need," Reed offered, and he hitched his thumb to the other deputy, Pete Nichols, who was already getting to his feet. "Pete'll be driving out there with you, and I'll make that call to your ranch hands to have a couple of them meet you at my house. If anything goes wrong, I can be out there in ten minutes."

It all sounded like a good plan, except for Elise. She wobbled, giving Colt two choices. He could carry her back to the flop room and let her sleep off the medication, or he could take Reed up on his offer.

"Joplin called," Reed added as if reading Colt's mind. "He's at the jail with Jewell right now but said he's heading up here when he's done."

Elise groaned, and Colt knew he'd get her out of there. Part of him wanted to stay, to confront Joplin and see if he could get the lawyer to back off, but Elise would still be able to hear that confrontation even if she stayed out of sight. Plus, he doubted he could say anything to make Joplin change his mind.

"Did Joplin petition to have me removed from Colt's custody?" Elise asked.

Reed nodded. "And he just might get it approved. Yet even more reason you should get the heck out of here," he added to Colt. "When Joplin shows, I don't intend to tell him where you are."

Good. Because Elise needed at least a few hours of peace and quiet. Heck, so did he.

"I'll follow in my truck," Pete said, following them to the door. "It's parked right next to yours."

"Thanks," Colt told both his fellow deputies. When this was over, he owed them, big-time. His brother, too, since Cooper had made protecting Elise a top priority.

Colt put on his coat, helped Elise with hers and he paused in the doorway. He had a look around. Nothing seemed out of place, but still he hurried as much as he could. He used his keypad to unlock the truck, and reached for the passenger's-side door so he could get Elise inside fast.

But his hand froze on the handle when he saw what was on the driver's seat.

Hell.

"Get down!" Colt yelled.

Chapter Thirteen

Elise was woozy, everything swimming in and out of focus, but she still managed to see what had caused Colt's reaction.

A gun rigged with some kind of device.

Colt ran, dragging her along with him, and he pulled her to the rear of the nearest vehicle—one parked on the side of the street by the parking lot. Not a second too soon. He'd barely gotten them on the ground when the shots started.

That jolted away some of the wooziness, and her heart slammed against her chest. Mercy, not this, not now.

"The gun's activated by remote control," Colt said, drawing his own weapon and crawling on top of her to protect her.

"Get down!" he shouted again.

Elise couldn't see anyone other than Pete, the deputy, and he'd taken cover on the side of a truck. He, too, had his gun drawn and ready, and like Colt, his gaze was firing all around them.

It hit her then that the gun in Colt's truck could be some kind of ruse to draw their attention away from the person who'd launched this attack.

Elise lifted her head a fraction to look around. Or at least she tried, but Colt put her right back down.

The shots continued, and even though she could no longer see Colt's truck, she could hear the bullets ripping through the door. If this was like the remote-control gun at her ranch, then the shots would be hitting the same spot. She prayed that spot wasn't the sheriff's office or any of the other nearby buildings.

This monster might be after her, but he or she could end up killing an innocent bystander.

Colt reached up and tested the door handle of the vehicle they were using for cover, but he cursed when it was locked. Maybe the owner would realize what was happening and open it from wherever he or she was.

That created another slam of fear inside her.

"What if this car is rigged to blow up or something?" she asked, though she wasn't sure how Colt could understand her with her words slurred and her voice shaking as hard as the rest of her.

"Any of the vehicles could blow up," he reminded her. "But this car doesn't belong to the shooter. It belongs to Herman Vinton, and he'll be in the diner this time of the morning."

That was something at least, but it didn't mean the shooter hadn't managed to get into Herman's car, as well.

"See anything?" Colt shouted to Pete.

"No. He might be on one of the roofs."

Mercy, there were plenty of them, including the sheriff's office itself. With all the activity going on inside the building, it was possible that no one had noticed the person who'd broken into Colt's truck and left that remote-control gun. Worse, the gun could have been put there during the night when no one would have been likely to see what was going on.

"The gun should run out of bullets soon," Colt said to her over the deafening blasts.

Elise could hear the frantic shouts and cries from the people in the diner across the street. At this time of morning, it was possible there were even schoolchildren out and about. But until the shots stopped firing, Colt and she were literally pinned down and unable to help.

It was hard to tell exactly where the shots were going, but, thankfully, it wasn't toward them or the other deputy. Also, other than the initial sound from Colt's truck window, she didn't hear any breaking glass.

Maybe that meant the shots weren't going into any of the buildings.

"Tell Reed we need eyes on the roofs," Colt shouted to Pete, and the deputy took out his phone to make a call. He was no doubt calling for some kind of backup, too, since they would need to search the entire area.

Maybe this time they'd get lucky.

Of course, the person who'd set all of this up could be just another hired gun like Martinelli. That meant any of their suspects could be responsible.

"Joplin would know about the restraining order I filed against him," she said. And Elise figured that certainly hadn't made him happy.

Had it caused him to do something like this?

Of course, this was also right up Buddy's alley. Meredith's, too, since her scummy brother could have done the dirty work for her.

The shots stopped. Finally. But Colt didn't move. He stayed on top of her, keeping watch. Protecting her—again. She hated that his life and so many others' were in danger because of her.

"Reed's making calls," Pete relayed. "Cooper and your brother Tucker are on their way to set up a roadblock."

Good. That might stop this idiot from escaping. If the person was still around, that is. With the shots silenced, there didn't seem to be any sign of their attacker. Of course, he could be waiting for them to leave cover so he'd be able to gun them down.

"I'm sorry," she whispered. "I shouldn't have insisted we leave the sheriff's office."

"Don't," Colt warned her. "He would have just found another way to come after us."

Colt was right, but that tightened the knot in her stomach. This monster wasn't going to stop until he killed Colt and her.

Colt's phone buzzed, and without taking his attention off their surroundings, he handed Elise the device so that she could no doubt read the text message that popped up on the screen.

"It's from Reed," she relayed. "He's going out the back of the sheriff's office so he can get a better look at the roofs."

"Good. Ask him to call Herman and see if he has a way of unlocking his car from the diner," Colt instructed.

Elise fired off the text to Reed. And waited. Her body bracing itself for yet another attack. At least if they were in the car, that would give them some small measure of protection.

But that idea quickly went south.

"'Herman doesn't have a remote key to unlock the car,'" she read aloud when Reed answered.

It was an older-model car so that wasn't surprising. But that meant they were stuck. It was a good twenty-five feet to get back into the sheriff's office. About the same distance to get into the diner. That was a lot of space where they'd be out in the open and vulnerable to an attack.

"As soon as Reed gives us the all clear," Colt said, "we'll move."

That couldn't come soon enough. But the seconds crawled by, turning into minutes. Colt and she had on coats, but it didn't take long for the cold from the pavement to seep through her clothes. She started to shiver.

"He's on the roof of the diner!" Pete shouted.

That was the only warning they got before the blast ripped through the air. This time, there was the sound of shattering glass because the shot blew out the window just above their heads.

"Get under the car," Colt insisted, but he was already shoving her in that direction.

It wasn't fast enough. More shots came, one slamming into the tire just inches from them.

"Keep moving," Colt told her. "Get to the other side of the car."

She scrambled over the rough pavement, but there wasn't a lot of room between Herman's car and the curb. Still, Elise managed to squeeze in, and she reached for Colt to pull him to safety.

Just as the hail of bullets started.

She could no longer see Pete, but she prayed he'd managed to get out of the way in time. Reed, too.

"Stay here," Colt ordered the moment he was fully out from beneath the car. He crawled toward the rear of the car, and using it for cover, took aim.

And fired.

Elise couldn't tell if he hit the shooter, but at least the bullets stopped. For a few seconds, anyway. Then they picked back up, and she realized the shooter had moved. Probably because Colt had come close to taking him out.

"There," Colt said, motioning to someone behind him.

Elise spotted both Reed and Pete on the side of the sheriff's office. They, too, had their weapons aimed at the roof of the diner, and both fired.

Again, the shots stopped.

And this time, they didn't immediately start back up.

"Hell, he's getting away," Colt said, and judging from his body language, he'd been about to bolt. No doubt to go in pursuit. But then he must have remembered she was there.

"It could be a trick," he added. "To get you alone." Colt mouthed some profanity and looked in the direction of the other deputies. "Reed, is it safe for you to move?" he asked.

Reed looked around, nodded, and he told Pete to cover him. Reed raced toward Herman's car and dropped to the pavement next to Colt.

"Guard Elise," Colt told Reed.

The deputy didn't question Colt's order, but Elise certainly did. "It's not safe. This could be a trick to draw you out."

"I'm not letting him get away again," Colt insisted, and he gave her a look. A warning, actually, for her to stay put, and he took off.

"He'll be okay," Reed told her, and he held her in place when she tried to lever herself up. But Reed didn't sound totally convinced of that.

And for a good reason.

The shooter on the roof had a much better vantage point than any of them. He could gun Colt down before he even made it across the street.

Pete didn't stay put, either. As Reed had done, he hurried toward the car and took cover behind the back bumper where Colt had just been.

"Did you get a look at the shooter?" she asked.

Pete shook his head, but Reed nodded. "A guy, but I couldn't see his face. Don't think it's anyone we know, though."

Then maybe she'd been right about it being a hired gun. Elise wanted to yell out to the guy that it hadn't turned out so well for the last person who'd been hired to do her harm. He'd been blown to bits. But yelling would only give away their exact position—if by some miracle the shooter didn't already know that.

Of course, a distraction might stop him from trying to take a shot at Colt.

She pulled off her shoe and hurled it over the front end of the car. It worked. Well, sort of. The guy did indeed fire a shot, and it slammed into the hood.

Reed cursed and shoved her flat on the pavement again.

"Colt won't be happy about you doing that," Reed told her.

No, but at least it'd pinpointed the position of the shooter, and it'd gotten his attention off Colt. Hopefully long enough for Colt to make it to cover so he could go after this guy.

"He's still on the roof," Pete said when a second shot came their way.

Pete levered himself up and returned fire, the blast so close to Elise that the sound of his gun shot through her head. Not good. She was still a little woozy, and she wanted a clear mind in case they had to escape or help Colt.

"Colt's using the Dumpster to get onto the roof,"

Reed relayed to her. And he, too, sent a shot the gunman's way. No doubt to keep him distracted so he wouldn't hear Colt trying to sneak up on him.

Elise held her breath and prayed some more. As much as she wanted the bullets to stop, the silence was even more chilling when they did.

Did that mean the shooter was onto Colt? He could be walking right into another trap.

"Go help him, please," Elise whispered to Reed.

But Reed quickly shook his head. "Colt will have my hide if I leave you."

He would, but they had to do something, anything. "Fire some more shots at the gunman to distract him."

Another head shake from Reed. "I can't fire any more shots because Colt just got on the roof."

Oh, mercy.

Elise had to see what was happening. Without lifting her head—something Reed obviously wouldn't have allowed her to do, anyway—she angled her body and looked up, craning her neck so she got a glimpse of the roof.

She didn't see anyone.

But she certainly heard something.

A gunshot.

Then another.

She couldn't tell if they'd come from Colt's gun, the shooter's. Or both. It was possible they'd fired and shot each other.

With that horrible thought racing through her head, she had to fight to make herself stay put. The seconds crawled by, and because she was listening so carefully, the next gun blast caused her to jump.

So did Reed.

He got to his feet, automatically aiming his gun at the roof. But the deputy didn't fire.

Elise got just a glimpse of the man falling. Before he crashed with a thud onto the street below.

Chapter Fourteen

Colt hated the fear he saw in Elise's eyes. Hated that he hadn't been able to stop the latest attack. Hated even more that he might not be able to stop another one.

It'd been a hellish long day what with the shooting, the mop-up from it and Elise's hypnosis session. Colt was hoping for a much more peaceful night.

"The guy's name is Arnold Levinson," Reed said.

Even though Colt didn't have the call on speaker, Elise was close enough so she could clearly hear every word the deputy was saying to him.

"Who was he?" she asked.

"A lowlife with a long record, but among other things he's done work as a bouncer," Reed answered, obviously not having any problems hearing Elise, either. "No connection that I can find to any of our suspects. But I'll keep looking," Reed added before Colt could ask him to do just that.

"Another hired gun," Elise mumbled. That got her pacing across Reed's kitchen while she scrubbed her hands up and down her arms. She probably wasn't cold since the house was toasty warm, but it might be a while before the chill left her.

If ever.

"Call me if you find out anything from our suspects," Colt added.

Since Reed had already said that he was bringing in Joplin and Meredith for questioning, he might learn something new. And while Colt was wishing, he added that maybe someone would find Buddy and haul his butt in, as well.

"It could have been you falling off that roof," Elise said the moment he finished the call with Reed. "It could have been you with a bullet to the chest."

"But it wasn't." He went to her, knowing that she would resist when he pulled her into his arms. She did. She was too wound up to stay still, but Colt held her, anyway. "You heard what Reed said. The guy was a lowlife not a pro."

He could thank his lucky stars for that. If the idiot had been a better shot, they might all be dead. Instead, the would-be killer was the one who'd been killed.

The remote-control device would be sent for testing, of course, and his truck would be dusted for prints and any other evidence that could be found connected to the break-in. That and all the other things they had in motion might help them ID this sack of dirt before he or she did any more harm.

Elise made a shivery sound of frustration, and Colt pulled her even closer. Yeah, it was dumb and dangerous. There was already enough tension left over from the attack without adding a different kind of tension. The kind that came from holding Elise in his arms.

That didn't stop him.

Colt figured the sweet torture was worth it if it gave her any comfort whatsoever. Of course, what was comfort for her would be another torture session for him.

"At least we won't have to deal with any surprise visits while we're here," Colt reminded her.

The security system was on and armed. Darnell, the ranch hand, had a gun and was in the living room at the front of the house, where he'd stay for the night. Plus, Reed's two dogs, Sampson and Delilah, were on the glassed-in porch at the back of the house. They were barkers, Reed had told them, and would alert them to anything.

Colt was counting heavily on that.

Still, even with all those measures and the fact that Elise was continuing to fight the effects of the sedative from the hypnosis session, Colt figured this would be yet another restless night. That was okay. He'd take restless over danger.

"You should go to bed," he reminded her—again. Like his other reminders, she stayed put as if somehow staying awake would protect them.

"Alone," Colt added when her eyebrow came up.

"Alone," she repeated, leaning into him.

She probably hadn't meant for her body to land against his like that. But it did. And Colt's body noticed, all right.

He quickly told those noticing parts to knock it off.

"Come on," he added, giving her a nudge toward the bedroom. "I brought the sleeping bag with me, and I can crash on the floor again."

Maybe.

But he figured that he'd get about as much sleep as Darnell and Elise. Little to none. Between keeping watch and reining in his body, it was going to be a long night.

She finally moved when Colt gave her another nudge and got her walking in the direction of Reed's guest room. The walls were decorated like a nursery in pale *yellow* with baby-duck decals. No doubt leftover decor from Reed's ex-wife, who, from all accounts, had desperately wanted a baby but hadn't been able to have one. Even though Reed obviously hadn't gotten around to redecorating since the divorce, he'd added a bed that looked freshly made and ready for Elise.

Not for Colt, though.

With everything they'd been through, getting into bed with her would lead to trouble. Even though his back was already protesting the hard floor and another part of him was protesting because it wasn't going to get lucky. The floor was where he'd spend the night keeping watch.

She didn't change into the gown that she'd brought from her house. Good thing. Best if she stayed covered so he couldn't see what he was missing. Instead, Elise dropped onto the bed, staring up at the ceiling. Colt turned off the light and did the same. He got onto the sleeping bag that he'd already rolled out.

"If I just leave town, disappear," Elise added. "Then I could hire a bodyguard. I could give a deposition for my testimony, and you and your family would be safe."

"*You* still wouldn't be safe," he reminded her.

But it was a moot point, anyway. He wasn't letting her leave. Yeah, it was probably cocky to feel this way, but he'd do a better job protecting her than some bodyguard for hire.

"What if it's never safe?" she asked. She rolled to the edge of the bed and looked down at him.

Best to put a lighter spin on this since even though he couldn't see her eyes in the darkness, he figured the fear was creeping back into them. Or maybe it'd never left.

"You don't have much faith in my abilities as a lawman, do you?" He didn't wait for her to answer. "Well, you should. I've been a deputy for nearly nine years now, and I've always done a good job with protection detail. Only been shot once."

She made a sharp sound of surprise. "You were shot?"

Heck, he figured her grandmother had told her all about that. Apparently not. So much for his attempt to lighten things up. Talking about gunshot wounds would do anything but.

"Sue Morgan's ex shot me when I was trying to break up a fight between them," he said, and he automatically rubbed what was now a faint scar on his abdomen. "Nothing serious."

Well, he'd nearly died, but best to keep that to himself, too.

"Whatever happens," she said, "I don't want you to step in front of a bullet for me. I'm already on your family's bad side. I'd rather not add personal injury or attempted personal injury to it."

Colt couldn't help it. He chuckled. "You're soon to be on their good side. Well, my brothers' good sides, anyway. You cleared our dad's name."

"Yes, that was something at least. Still, stay out of the path of bullets. And don't go charging up on any other roofs to get bad guys."

"Uh, that's kind of my job description."

She stared down at him. Now that his eyes had adjusted to the dark room, he could see that her own eyes were narrowed a bit. Elise obviously wasn't happy that he would put himself in danger for her.

But he would.

"Okay," he said to placate her. And hopefully to get her to go to sleep. "No charging after bad guys."

Not until it was absolutely necessary, that is.

"Good." She mumbled something else that he didn't catch and dropped back down on the bed. "Here we are sleeping under the same roof again. You can bet Joplin will try to use this against me in some way."

Yeah, he would. "He might try," Colt settled for saying.

That brought her to the edge of the bed again, and he expected the conversation to continue. After all, Elise no doubt had plenty of fears and concerns that she needed calming.

Or not.

That wasn't exactly a soothe-me look she had in her eyes now.

Elise eased off the bed and landed next to him on the floor. "This can work two ways," she said. "I can throw myself at you, and you can crush me by saying no. Or—"

Colt didn't need to hear the other part of that. Because there was zero chance of his saying no. Even if that's exactly what he should be saying.

He slipped his hand around the back of her neck, pulled her to him and kissed her. This might not help their situation, but he figured it would help them. For a little while, anyway.

She slipped right into the kiss. Right against him, too, and put her arms around him to pull him even closer. Not that he wasn't already heading in that direction, anyway, but she closed the already narrow gap between their bodies.

Colt took things from there. He deepened the kiss. Felt that punch of heat that he knew would be there. Then felt it burn even hotter. It made him wonder how he'd been able to go so long resisting this. Resisting her.

"I should give you an out," he whispered.

"I don't want one." And she pulled him right back to her for yet another kiss.

It was just as good as the first kiss, but there was a big problem with kisses like that. They only caused the heat to rise higher and higher until soon kissing wasn't nearly enough.

Colt slid his hand beneath her sweater, unhooked her bra, and her breasts spilled into his hands. No way could he resist that, so he shoved up her top and moved the kisses from her mouth to her nipples.

Elise obviously liked that.

She made a silky sound of pleasure, threaded her fingers through his hair and let him feast on her. It was just as good as the kisses, too, but soon it wasn't enough, either.

Elise tried to do something about that. She went after his shirt and would have managed to shove it off if his shoulder holster hadn't gotten in the way. Colt had to stop the breast kisses to help her unhook it. The holster and gun went on the floor next to them, followed by his shirt.

Then, her sweater.

He got another punch of that burning need when her bare skin landed against his. He'd thought about being with her like this for years. Since they'd shared that first kiss way back when, and those years hadn't diminished the need one little bit. He still wanted her—bad.

"Let's finish this," she insisted.

He had no plans to argue with that, either.

Colt rid her of her jeans. It wasn't a pretty maneuver, and the need made them fumble, but they grappled enough to get his jeans off, too.

And then he remembered the stitches on her head.

Something he should have considered before he even started kissing her.

"I don't want to hurt you," he said.

She blinked, as if trying to figure out what that meant. Maybe she was thinking about all the emotional fallout they'd have from this.

"Your head," he added.

"Oh." She sounded relieved and kissed him again. "You won't hurt me."

Colt wasn't so sure of that at all, especially since that latest kiss upped the ante tenfold. So did stripping off her panties. Ditto for his touching her in the center of all that heat.

Oh, man.

She was hot, wet and ready.

And even though his mind kept telling him to slow down and be gentle, they were well past that stage.

Colt gathered her beneath him and sank into her.

The sound that Elise made was one of relief. Then, pure pleasure. It was a sound that slammed through him, and coupled with the feel of being inside her, there was no way Colt couldn't do what she'd demanded.

Finish this.

He moved inside her. Elise moved with him. It was perfect. But perfect meant this would all end a heck of a lot sooner than he wanted.

Still, Colt had no choice. His body was in control now, and it drove him to take her. To push her toward the only place either of them wanted to go.

It didn't take much. She was so ready that he felt that climax ripple through her. And in that moment, the moonlight landed on her face. So beautiful. As perfect as the moment.

That couldn't last.

Colt pushed into her one last time, releasing them both from the blazing fire.

ELISE HAD TO catch onto Colt to stop him from immediately moving off her.

"Your stitches," he reminded her again.

"Aren't bothering me in the least," she assured him.

It was somewhat of a miracle. She'd been in pain for two days, ever since the attack that'd resulted in the stitches, but sex with Colt seemed to be the cure for even the worst pain.

However, it obviously wasn't a cure for Colt.

He brushed one of those chaste kisses on her cheek and eased off her, dropping next to her on the sleeping bag. "I didn't use a condom," he murmured.

She was surprised that he could think of anything at the moment. Her brain was still a nice whirl of pleasure and other post-sex sensations. "I'm on the pill, remember?"

He no doubt did since she'd made such a big deal of personally getting them from her place.

But maybe this wasn't about the lack of condom. Maybe this was about the other thing that'd she been sure would surface.

"You're already regretting this," she said.

Colt stiffened and turned on his side so he could look at her. "No. That's the problem. I'm not regretting it at all, and I should be." He gave a heavy sigh. "It's best to keep a clear head in the middle of an attempted-murder investigation." He slipped his hand between them, touched her breast. "This doesn't equal clear head."

His touch gave her a nice little shiver of pleasure. Enough so that she wondered if she could coax him into another round. Well, maybe not if he was trying to keep a clear head.

"So, you're sure there are no regrets?" she clarified.

"Maybe one." He swiped his thumb over her nipple, causing another of those nice little waves of heat to race through her. "I should have made it last longer."

So, not the kind of regrets that she was worried about. Still, Elise didn't want him to feel hemmed in by what was essentially an old attraction.

But she rethought that.

Yes, it was an old one. But this didn't exactly feel old.

Oh, no.

Not this. Not with Colt.

However, *this* was exactly what was happening.

She wasn't just falling for him. She was falling in love with him.

"Are you in pain?" he quickly asked, levering himself up. "You made a funny sound."

No way would she tell him that sound involved the *L*-word. That would send a man like Colt running.

Before tonight, it might have sent her running, too. She'd always worked so hard to create her own life. And not one that she'd necessarily been born into. That was the reason she'd steered away from serious relationships. That, and no man had ever quite lived up to the one she'd left behind.

Colt.

"I'm fine," she lied.

But she wasn't. This really put a crimp in the plans she had. Getting a ranch up and running would take plenty of time and hard work. Elise certainly hadn't factored in a complicated relationship.

And with Colt, it would be complicated.

Even though she could essentially clear his father's

name, that wouldn't put her in the good graces of Colt's sister Rayanne, who had no doubt hoped that Elise's testimony would put the blame on anyone but Jewell. Heaven knew how long it'd take to mend fences with her. And with Jewell herself.

"So, what's wrong?" Colt asked. "Because you're being even quieter than I am."

Elise was about to turn the tables on him and ask him about that quietness. However, the quietness disappeared in a flash.

The dogs started barking.

The sound echoed through the house. Through her. And it brought both of them to their feet. They immediately started scrambling to put on their clothes.

"It might be nothing," Colt reminded her. "Reed said the dogs will bark at anything."

But Elise figured with their luck, it wasn't just anything. It was *something*. Or worse—some*one*.

"Darnell, I'll be out there in a second," Colt called out to the ranch hand. He zipped his jeans and put on his shoulder holster and gun. "You see anything?"

"Not yet," Darnell answered.

The dogs didn't stop. In fact, their barking got even louder, and Elise could tell they were on the side of the porch that was farther from the bedroom.

The moment Colt finished dressing, he threw open the door. "Stay away from the windows," he reminded her. "And don't turn on the lights."

With his gun drawn and ready, he hurried to join the ranch hand.

Elise pulled on the rest of her clothes and stepped into the dark hallway. Listening. But the only things she could hear were the dogs and Colt and Darnell's mumbled conversation.

She eased closer, keeping her footsteps light so she wouldn't disturb them, and she found both men in the living room. Darnell was looking out the front window, and Colt, out the side one. They weren't standing directly in front of the glass but, rather, were peering around the window edges.

Elise held her breath. Waiting. Something she'd been doing a lot of lately. For the past couple of days, her life had been filled with one attack after another.

Well, with the exception of making love with Colt.

That'd been a wonderful reprieve, but Colt would no doubt blame himself for that lapse in focus.

"I think I got something," Colt said, and that sent Darnell scurrying to the side window with Colt.

But Darnell shook his head when he had a look.

"In the pasture near the fence," Colt added.

Elise wasn't that familiar with Reed's ranch. She'd only gotten glimpses of it when they'd driven in because Colt had been so anxious to get her inside. However, she remembered the fenced side pasture that led to a small corral area and a barn. If someone was out there, they were already very close to the house.

And the dogs confirmed that.

Their barking became even more frantic, and it sounded as if they were trying to get out of the glassed-in porch so they could go after whoever was out there.

"Should I let the dogs out?" Darnell asked.

Colt shook his head. "No. If the person's armed, I don't want the dogs hurt. Besides, I'd rather them stay put in case there's an attempted break-in."

Oh, mercy. That really didn't help with her nerves. It was bad enough having someone so close, but she definitely didn't want another hired gun getting into the house. And it wasn't much of a stretch to believe the person behind the attacks would just hire someone to come after her since there were already two dead hit men who'd tried and failed.

"There," Colt said, pointing toward someone on the left side of the window. "Did you see it that time?"

Darnell didn't jump to answer. Then she saw the muscles in his body tense. "Yeah."

Elise didn't go closer, but she looked over their shoulders out into the night landscape. There was still a full moon, plenty light enough for her to see something she definitely didn't want to see.

A man.

Elise caught just a glimpse of him as he ducked behind the barn. But a glimpse was all she needed to see that the man was armed with a rifle.

Chapter Fifteen

"Elise, get down on the floor now," Colt ordered her.

She was already headed in that direction, which meant she had no doubt seen the latest threat outside the window. The armed guy less than twenty yards from the house. Hard to miss him with the moonlight glinting off the barrel of his rifle.

Darnell and Colt both took aim at the man, but since he was using the barn for cover, they didn't have a clean shot. But once they did, it was a shot that Colt would take. He doubted this was a neighborly visit at this hour, and with all the mess that Elise and he had been through, he didn't intend to take any more chances.

Colt fired off a text to Reed and his brother requesting backup ASAP and hoped Reed had been right about it not taking them long to get out there. With the gunman already in place, they didn't have much time.

The dogs continued to bark, and Colt wondered if that was the reason the guy was staying back. The Dobermans sounded ready to tear someone limb from limb, and probably would if they got the chance. It might just stop this idiot from trying to break in.

"Is it just one man?" Elise asked him.

"Yeah."

But Colt wasn't holding out hope that the guy had

come alone. If the person who wanted her dead was as desperate as Colt figured he was, there could be several hired guns out there hiding somewhere.

"Go to the kitchen and keep watch," he told Darnell just in case someone tried to sneak up on them from that direction. If that happened, hopefully the dogs would move to that side of the porch so they'd have some warning.

That thought had no sooner crossed his mind when the dogs did exactly that. He heard the Dobermans scramble to the other side. No longer focused just on the pasture, something else had obviously alerted them. Something on the very side where he'd just sent Darnell.

"I don't see anyone," Darnell called out.

Hell.

Colt hadn't meant to curse out loud because he didn't want to alarm Elise more than she already was. But she obviously heard his profanity and knew what it meant. That they might be right in the middle of an ambush, and if they couldn't even pinpoint their attackers, there was no way to prevent something bad from happening.

"I can keep watch out front," she said. "And I'll stay down and back from the windows."

Colt wanted to refuse, but the truth was, he needed her eyes and ears right now. Between Darnell and him, they had the sides and the back covered, but someone could use the road directly in front of the house to get to them.

"Cooper or Reed should arrive in the next five minutes," Colt told her.

She nodded, moved to the wall between the front door and a window.

"I've got a guy behind some trees," Darnell called out. "I'm pretty sure he's got a rifle, too."

Yes, that's what Colt figured, too. With rifles, the shooters wouldn't have to get too close to the house to do some serious damage.

But what were they waiting for?

With the dogs, they'd clearly lost any element of surprise, and they had to know that Colt and anyone else inside would be armed and ready. Colt immediately thought of a bad reason why they hadn't already started to shoot up the place.

Maybe they were waiting on even more firepower.

Until he'd realized that, Colt had been about to text Reed and tell him to make a quiet approach. So that perhaps they would stand a chance at catching these guys and could get information from them. But no way could that happen now. Colt wanted sirens blaring in an effort to scare off these idiots.

"The guy behind the tree isn't moving," Darnell said at the same time that Elise spoke up. "There's someone driving up the road toward us. It's an SUV, but the headlights are off."

"It is Reed or Cooper?" Colt asked.

Elise leaned in closer to the window, prompting Colt to order her to stay back. She did but then shook her head. "I don't think it's Reed or your brother. I don't recognize the vehicle."

Great. They were coming at them from all angles now, and Colt still didn't know how many were out there.

"There's a gun on the top of Reed's fridge," Colt told her. "Get it."

Even though he hated the thought of Elise being put in a position where she might have to pull the trigger. Still, he had to be reasonable here and give her a way to defend herself if the worst happened. Especially since plenty of *worst* had already happened to them.

Elise scurried into the kitchen, and it took her only a few seconds before she returned to the window. "The SUV stopped on the side of the road," she relayed. "No, wait. It's pulling off the road and into some bushes."

No doubt so it'd be out of sight. Maybe in place to ambush anyone who came to help. While Colt kept an eye on the guy by the barn, he sent a text to Reed to let him know what was going on.

"Reed's not far out," Colt relayed to Elise and Darnell as soon as he got a response from his fellow deputy.

The seconds crawled by, and Colt hoped that Reed's presence would be enough to send these guys scattering. Maybe then he could pick off one of them and arrest the sorry piece of dirt.

"The car door opened," Elise said. "Someone got out, but I can't see who. I think he's heading toward the guy behind the trees."

So, three of them. At least.

Finally, Colt heard a sound that he wanted to hear. Reed was obviously close by, and he had the sirens blaring at max volume.

Elise blew out what sounded to be a breath of relief, but Colt didn't do the same. That's because the guy behind the barn moved.

And not just moved.

The man leaned out and fired a shot directly at Colt.

THE BULLET CRASHED through the window, sending a spray of glass all over the room. And right at Colt.

"Get down!" Elise shouted, praying he wouldn't get hurt.

Colt didn't listen. However, he did bolt from the window and ran toward her. He hooked his arm around her waist and pulled her to the floor.

Not a second too soon.

Because another bullet blasted through what was left of the window. Unlike the shots that'd been rigged with the remote control, the angles were totally different on these, which meant they had a real shooter on their hands.

And it was obvious this guy was trying to kill them.

With his arm still around her, Colt crawled with her toward the kitchen. She spotted Darnell, not on the floor, but he'd taken aim at the window where he'd been keeping watch. However, before Colt and she could even reach him, a bullet tore through the kitchen window.

Then through the front door.

Sweet heaven.

All three gunmen were shooting at them, and they were trapped in the middle with no way out.

"If anyone opens a door or window, the alarm will sound," Colt reminded her.

It was good that they'd get a warning, but Elise figured it was possible for those bullets to damage the security system. Then, while they were busy defending themselves and dodging gunfire, one of the shooters could sneak into the house.

Colt pushed her to the side of the fridge door. Probably because it was as safe a place as they could manage right now. She reached to pull him down with her, but he went to the window, and both Darnell and he returned fire.

The dogs had worked themselves into a frenzy now, and she could hear them trying to claw their way out. Maybe the gunmen would stay away from there because it was too dangerous for someone to go back to the glassed-in porch to check on the animals.

Colt fired off another shot, pulled back, and this time the gunman's bullet tore into the wall just above her head.

"They're using cop killers," Colt told her.

Her heart was already bashing against her ribs, and that didn't help. "What?" she asked.

"Teflon-coated bullets," Colt answered while he volleyed his attention between the front door and the window. "They'll be able to go through the walls of this old house."

It didn't take long for her to realize just how true that was. The bullets coming through the front door were tearing through the half wall that separated the living room from the kitchen. With the shots coming from both sides of the house, it wouldn't be long before the place was ripped to pieces.

"Reed won't be able to get closer with all this gunfire," Darnell added.

Elise prayed that he didn't try, either. As much as she wanted help, she didn't want anyone else's life put at stake because of her, and Reed would definitely be in grave danger if he tried to get to them now.

More bullets came. Nonstop. And Colt and Darnell had no choice but to drop down on the floor next to her. They were literally pinned down and with no way to fight back. If they stood up to return fire, one of those cop-killer bullets could take them out.

"We have to move," Colt said, glancing all around him. "If we go out the back, they'll probably just gun us down."

That definitely was not an option that Elise wanted. But he was right, they had to move. At the rate those bullets were coming, soon there wouldn't be enough of the walls left to give them any cover.

Colt's attention landed on the small utility room that divided the kitchen from the porch where the dogs were closed off. Except he wasn't looking at the door that led to the porch. He was looking at the ceiling.

"Come on." Colt took hold of her hand. "There's an attic. If we can get up there, Darnell and I will have a better chance at picking these guys off."

An attic definitely sounded better to her than staying put, but bullets could go through the utility room as well as they could any other part of the house.

Colt didn't waste any time getting them moving. They stayed on the floor, crawling, and he didn't stand up until he'd made it all the way to the laundry room. He pulled down the wooden attic stairs and climbed up to have a look around.

Elise got a new slam of concern. What if someone was up there waiting? The security alarm hadn't gone off, but maybe one of the gunmen had managed to get on the roof and climb into the attic. She doubted the security system was armed for that part of the house.

"It's clear," Colt said.

Thank God. And he motioned for Darnell and her to follow him.

The steps were narrow and wobbly, but with Colt's help, Elise made it to the top and into the attic. However, once Darnell was there, Colt went back down, causing her adrenaline to spike again.

To release the dogs, she soon realized.

The moment he opened the door of the porch, the barking Dobermans charged through the house.

"Stay," Colt ordered, and Elise was surprised when they sat on the laundry room floor and obeyed. Maybe since they were now sitting down low enough, that would keep them out of the line of fire.

Colt came back up and then pulled up the stairs behind him. No doubt so if the shooters got into the house, they wouldn't be able to find them right away. Still, she wasn't sure it would fool a determined killer for long.

Darnell hurried to the small wooden ventilation window that was at the front of the attic, and he looked out. "I see one of them," he relayed to Colt a moment later. "And I think we're close enough to take the shot."

Good. Elise hated the thought of anyone being killed, but she didn't want the gunmen to have a chance to kill them. And that's exactly what would happen if they got the chance. The other attacks had proved that.

Darnell stepped to the side once Colt made it to the window, and Elise stayed back as Colt did a quick assessment of the situation. He bashed through the wooden slats with the butt of his gun, and without wasting even a second, he took aim.

And he fired.

The problem was that the shooter fired, too, and the shots blasted through the air at seemingly the same time. Colt ducked down, waited a few seconds and then had another look.

"Got him," Colt said. "One down, at least two to go." He moved to the other side of the window, no doubt looking for the shooter who'd been near the kitchen.

But the sound stopped him.

An alarm.

And Elise immediately knew what that meant. Someone had triggered the security system and was in the house.

Oh, mercy.

If the gunman came up the stairs, they could be in the middle of another shoot-out.

She heard something else. Maybe a door opening. And a moment later, the dogs bolted outside into the front yard. Still barking, they raced toward the SUV that was parked just up the road. Several moments later, both Dobermans disappeared into the trees.

Then, Elise heard something else she didn't want to hear. Something that caused her heart to skip a beat or two.

The dogs stopped barking.

There'd been no gunshots, so maybe the intruder had used some kind of Taser on them. She hoped that's all that had happened, anyway, especially since the dogs had saved their lives by alerting them of the first intruder. Without their warning, the gunman could have gotten close enough to do some serious damage while Colt and she were still in the guest bedroom.

"Stay back," Colt whispered to her.

He moved in front of her and lifted his head, obviously trying to pick through the clamor of the security alarm so he could try to pinpoint the location of their intruder.

But it didn't take long to hear something.

Footsteps.

And they were headed straight for the stairs below them.

Chapter Sixteen

Hell. Colt had hoped that by going up into the attic it would keep those bullets away from Elise.

Now the shooter could be coming for them.

It wouldn't take the intruder long to search the place, and once he realized they weren't in any of the rooms of the one-story house, then the attic would be the most obvious hiding place. Especially since they hadn't gone outside. Plus, these goons likely figured out that the shot Colt had fired had come from the attic.

If the shooter came up the stairs, they'd be trapped.

Colt couldn't move Elise to the sides or front of the attic because there might be gunmen in place ready to start firing at them. All he could do was stand in front of her and keep his gun ready. The moment the guy surfaced on the stairs, Colt would have to fire.

The seconds crawled by with each step the gunman took. Thanks to the creaky floors, Colt had no trouble hearing the guy even over the security alarm. However, he also heard something else.

His phone buzzed.

Not exactly a good time for a call, but it might be Reed or Cooper phoning to warn them of something.

"See who it is," Colt whispered to Elise, and he angled his body so that she could take his cell from his jeans pocket.

"It's Rosalie," Elise answered in a whisper as soon as she checked the phone screen.

His sister was the last person that Colt expected to be calling him, but since he didn't want Elise or himself distracted by the call, he let it go to voice mail. Maybe soon he'd get a chance to call Rosalie back—after he had Elise and Darnell safely out of this mess.

Downstairs, the sound of the footsteps stopped, and Colt braced himself for the attack that he was certain would follow. His heartbeat was already hammering in his ears. His muscles tightened and knotted. He was ready to finish this.

But the shooter didn't pull down the stairs so he could come into the attic.

In fact, it sounded as if this idiot was just standing still.

What the heck was he doing down there?

"Don't move," Colt warned both Elise and Darnell, keeping his voice as soundless as possible. "The guy might be listening for us so he can shoot through the ceiling."

If so, they had to be prepared to move and move fast.

The problem was, there weren't many places for them to go in the attic, especially since there was at least one other gunman outside the house. In hindsight, it'd been a mistake to bring Elise up here, but they hadn't exactly had a lot of options about that, either. If they'd stayed on the bottom floor of the house, one of them could have been shot.

Without warning, the security alarm stopped, plunging the house into an eerie quiet. Since Colt doubted it operated on a battery, that probably meant someone had managed to disable it either by cutting the connections or the phone line.

That was both good and bad.

Colt could better hear the shooter, but the shooter could better hear them, too. Also, without the alarm, Colt got a confirmation of something he'd already suspected.

The dogs were quiet.

It meant these goons could have neutralized them in some way. Or maybe, though, they'd made it safely to Reed. His fellow deputy had to be somewhere nearby, and the dogs would have picked up his scent. If so, Reed would have made sure they were safe.

Reed could also do something else.

He'd know the ins and outs of the grounds. Maybe he'd even be able to sneak up on the gunman outside.

But that still left Colt to deal with the one inside.

Why wasn't he moving?

Colt wasn't a patient man under normal circumstances, but this was wearing his nerves even thinner than they already were.

He mumbled some profanity when his phone buzzed again. This time, indicating that he had a text. Colt only hoped the shooter hadn't heard the buzzing sound so he could use it to zoom in on them.

"It's Rosalie again," Elise whispered. "She says it's urgent and that she needs to talk to you."

Well, his urgency trumped Rosalie's, but with everything else that'd been going on, Colt had no trouble filling in some blanks with worst-case scenarios. Maybe his sister was calling to say there'd been some kind of attack at the ranch.

If so, his family could be in serious danger.

"Text her back," Colt mouthed to Elise. "Ask her what's wrong."

Elise started to do that, but her hand froze when they heard the noise on the floor below them. It was hard to tell what it was exactly, but it sounded as if someone had dropped something metal.

Colt waited, listening for more, but that was it. Just that brief metallic sound. It took several moments for the footsteps to start again, but this time they weren't coming toward the attic stairs.

But rather toward the front of the house.

He motioned for Darnell to head back to the window, and the man cursed as soon as he looked out. Colt cursed, too, because he heard the front door open.

"The guy ran out," Darnell said, and he took aim and fired, the shot blasting through the attic.

Colt could tell from Darnell's body language that he'd missed, and the ranch hand fired again.

"I smell smoke," Elise said, lifting her head.

Colt didn't. Not at first, anyway. But then he caught a whiff of it making its way through the seam around the stairs.

Oh, man.

That metallic sound was likely some kind of incendiary device, and the reason the guy had run was because he'd just set the place on fire.

"We need to get out of here," Colt said, taking hold of Elise's arm. "Now."

ELISE SHOVED COLT'S phone into her jeans pocket so that it'd free up her hands in case she had to help shoot their way out of the house.

And that's almost certainly what would happen.

Unless their attackers meant to burn them alive.

Then this was probably a way to force them outside where the two remaining shooters would have an easier time picking them off. Of course, if they stayed put, the fire and smoke would kill them, too, so either way they were in grave danger.

Colt hurried across the attic and threw down the attic stairs. However, he didn't bolt down them. Instead, he looked around. Hard to see, though, with the thick white smoke already billowing through the house.

"Wait here a second," Colt told both of them.

Even though she hated that Colt was the one to go down the stairs first, Elise knew he wouldn't have it any other way. He was the lawman now. Fully in charge. And he would take any risk to try to protect her.

With his gun ready, Colt eased down several of the narrow steps, his gaze shifting all around. Almost immediately, he started to cough, and he had to cover his mouth with the sleeve of his shirt while he continued to make sure their attackers weren't still inside the house.

Elise and Darnell coughed, too, the smoke coming right at them. What she didn't feel was any kind of heat, though, so maybe that meant the place wasn't actually on fire. That metallic *plinging* sound she'd heard earlier could have perhaps been some kind of smoke bomb. If so, it would serve the same purpose as a full-fledged fire in getting them out of the house.

"Move fast," Colt said, motioning for them to come down the stairs.

Elise tried to do just that, but the stairs were wobbly, and her grip was shaking on the flimsy rope handrail. The coughing certainly didn't help, either. Still, she made it to the bottom with Darnell right behind her.

"This way," Colt added.

The moment they hit the floor, Colt got them running, not toward the back porch, which was closer. But toward the front of the house. Maybe because he figured that's the exit their attackers were least likely to use. It was also the place where Reed would be approaching.

They were all coughing now, and it got worse with each step. Elise's eyes and throat were burning, and she felt as if her lungs were on fire. It also didn't help that her heart was bashing against her ribs. Still, she kept moving.

Colt paused again when they reached the front door, and he eased it open. Elise held her breath, praying that someone didn't open fire on them.

No shots.

In fact, no sounds at all.

So, Colt opened the door a little farther.

Just the small crack of space brought in some fresh air. It helped with her breathing, but some of the smoke was also on the porch. It wasn't thick, just white wisps coiling around, but since someone had also knocked out the porch light, it was next to impossible to see beyond the steps that led into the front yard.

No doubt the way their attackers had planned it.

"We need a distraction," Colt said, glancing back at Darnell. "Fire a shot toward the back porch. It might get them focused there so we can make a run for it. Just as soon as you've pulled the trigger, we'll all run to the side of the porch and drop down into those shrubs."

Colt tipped his head to their right. To the side of the house where he'd already taken out the shooter. Of course, that didn't mean that the person who'd orchestrated this hadn't already put someone else in place, but it was still their best bet.

"Fire now," Colt told Darnell.

Because Darnell was so close to her, Elise covered

her ears for the brief second that it took him to get off the shot.

Then they moved.

Fast.

Colt took hold of her arm, and with Darnell right behind them, they bolted toward the side of the porch.

Just as the shot came their way.

The bullet slammed into the front of the house, but Colt didn't stop to return fire. He pulled her off the porch and into some Texas sage bush. The branches tore at her clothes and skin, but they all managed to get off the porch and into the meager cover before there were more shots.

Colt moved in front of her, of course.

He shoved her against the concrete slab and exterior wall. It was hard for her to see much of anything, what with the smoke and the darkness, but Elise thought the gunfire was coming from the front of the house. Maybe from the person who'd gotten out of that SUV parked just up the road?

However, that thought had no sooner crossed her mind when the angle of the shot changed.

The shooter was moving.

Coming for them.

Even over the thick blasts, she heard Colt's phone buzz again, and she fished it from her pocket so she could see the screen.

Rosalie again.

Something had to be seriously wrong for Colt's sister to keep calling and texting. Of course, Rosalie had no way of knowing that they were fighting for their lives right now.

Since Elise hadn't gotten to send the text when they were in the attic, she sent it now, asking Rosalie what she wanted. The moment she pressed the send button, Colt nudged her again.

"Start crawling toward the back," he told her, "but stay as close to the house as possible."

Thankfully, the line of Texas sage bush went all the way to the back porch, but Elise knew there wouldn't be any protection whatsoever against bullets. Still, the thick shrubs might keep the shooter from seeing them.

With Colt ahead of her and Darnell behind her, they started crawling. The ground was frozen and littered with small rocks and dried twigs that dug into her hands and knees. Still, Elise kept moving.

It seemed to take an eternity to go the ten yards or so, but once they reached the back porch, Colt stopped and looked around again. Just ahead was a storage shed, and he motioned toward it. At least she thought he was motioning, but then she realized he threw a handful of rocks at it.

Nothing.

No one came out with guns blazing, and even though the shooter was continuing to fire, those shots were going toward the front part of the house.

For now, anyway.

She figured that would soon change when he realized they'd moved. Or maybe when *she* realized they'd moved. After all, it was possible that Meredith was the one orchestrating this. If so, Elise hoped she got the chance to give the woman—or anyone else behind this—some payback.

First, though, Colt, Darnell and she had to survive.

Just as she'd known would happen, the angle of the shots changed again. The shooter was coming their way.

"We'll move to the left side of the shed," Colt said.

"Don't fire unless you have to, because we don't have a lot of ammo."

Mercy, she hadn't even considered that. These monsters had likely brought an arsenal with them, but Colt, Darnell and she only had the weapons in their hands. Not exactly an equal gunfight, especially since Elise wasn't even sure she could fire straight enough to help. Still, that wouldn't stop her from trying.

"Stay low and start moving to the shed," Colt instructed.

But almost immediately, he stopped and lifted his hand, a signal for them to stay put.

Elise followed his gaze to see what'd captured his attention. Colt was focused on a woodpile only about ten feet from the shed. She didn't see anything, but Colt obviously had, because even though the shooter was getting closer, he still didn't move.

Colt's phone buzzed again, indicating that someone had texted. Probably Rosalie, but Elise didn't want to look down to respond. Instead, both Darnell and she kept their guns lifted in case they had to fire.

"Hell," Colt said, his attention still on the woodpile.

Elise finally saw something. Some movement at the end of the pile nearest the shed.

Mercy, was it another gunman waiting there?

If so, he would have shot them before they could have made it out into the yard.

But the person didn't shoot. However, he did move again, because Elise got a glimpse of the sleeve of his jacket.

"Maybe it's Reed," Darnell said.

Judging from Colt's body language, it wasn't, but Elise couldn't tell who it was. Not until he moved again, that is.

The person ducked his head out from the woodpile for just a glimpse at them. But it was more than enough for Elise to get a glimpse of him.

What the devil was *he* doing here?

Chapter Seventeen

Buddy.

Colt had figured it was either Buddy, Meredith or Joplin behind these attacks, but he hadn't expected Elise's former tenant to actually take part in the shootings.

Especially since he had so many hired guns to do the job. From Colt's estimate there were still at least two of them out there somewhere.

"Don't shoot me," Buddy called out to them. "I'm here to help you."

Right. No way was Colt going to buy that.

After all, Buddy was wanted for murder, and he hated Elise for refusing to sell him the place where he'd buried the body. He no doubt blamed Elise for the trip he'd be making to jail, and that gave him plenty of motive for this attack.

"Somebody wanted me to kill Elise," Buddy went on. "I got a call. I couldn't make out who it was, but the caller said if I came here tonight, I could settle the score with Elise. I figured I was supposed to murder her, but that's not why I'm here. I never meant to kill that woman, and I don't want to kill Elise, either."

Colt glanced back at her to see if she was buying any of this. She wasn't. Elise had her gun aimed right at the woodpile where Buddy was hiding.

"You hear me, Colt?" Buddy asked.

Colt didn't answer because the sound of his voice would make it too easy to pinpoint their location. But there was some movement in the backyard on the other side of the shed.

Oh, man.

One of the shooters was no doubt moving closer. It was the same for the one at the front of the house. And that made it too risky to try to move Elise and Darnell to the shed.

"Get down as low as you can," Colt told her.

He positioned himself in front of her, but he knew he wouldn't be much protection if the bullets started coming at them from all directions.

"Colt?" someone called out. Not Buddy this time.

Reed.

Judging from the sound of Reed's voice, he was somewhere near the front of the house, too. Good. Maybe he'd be able to take out the shooter.

Or maybe he already had.

Colt realized it'd been a minute or so since anyone had fired a shot. Reed could have sneaked up on him and clubbed the guy. Colt hoped so, anyway, because he wanted to focus his attention on Buddy and on getting Elise to safety.

Wherever *safety* was.

"More help's on the way," Reed said. "Plenty of it."

Good. Colt wished he could bring in an army to stop these dirtbags.

"Text me your location," Reed added.

Just as another shot was fired.

That one went in Reed's direction.

"Text him," Colt whispered to Elise. "Tell him our location. The shooters. And Buddy's, too."

She gave a shaky nod and used his phone to fire off the text. Maybe Reed would be able to use the info to get himself in a better position to attack. Maybe, too, Reed would stay out of the line of fire.

Because it continued.

More shots came. Not just from the front but from the back side of the house. The shooter over there had obviously moved since they'd last spotted him from the kitchen window.

"I said don't shoot!" Buddy yelled, and he added a long string of raw profanity.

Buddy obviously thought Colt was doing the firing, or he wanted to make them believe he thought that. Colt still wasn't about to give away their position by answering him.

"Reed's going to try to get closer to the woodpile," Elise relayed when she got the text response from the deputy. "Cooper's at the end of the road, and he's going on the opposite side of the house from Reed."

Colt was more than thankful for the backup, but it meant Darnell or he wouldn't be able to fire any more random shots. He couldn't risk hitting Reed or his brother.

The shots continued to come, some of them aimed at the woodpile. Either this was another ploy to get them to trust Buddy, or these shooters wanted him dead, too.

Buddy cursed again, and he leaned out. That's when Colt saw the rifle, but Buddy didn't aim it at them. He pointed it in the area just past the shed, an area that was out of Colt's line of sight.

And Buddy fired.

Colt heard a sharp groan of pain, and it sounded as if someone collapsed onto the ground.

Hell. That could be his brother.

"Text Cooper now," Colt told Elise.

And Colt held his breath, waiting and praying. Thankfully, it only took a few seconds for Cooper to respond.

"Cooper's okay," Elise said, blowing out her own breath of relief. "Buddy shot one of the gunmen."

Good. But again it could be a ploy to get them to trust him and come out in the open. That wasn't going to happen.

"If Reed can neutralize Buddy, I can get you into the shed," Colt whispered to her.

Of course, if Reed took out Buddy, and Cooper got the guy who'd been at the front of the house, there would be no need for Elise to be in the shed. The danger would be over.

He hoped.

And that meant they needed to keep Buddy alive so they could get any other details of the attack. One way or another, Colt wanted to end the danger tonight.

His phone buzzed again, and Colt hoped it was a message with good news from Reed or Cooper. However, judging from the way Elise pulled in her breath, it wasn't.

"It's another message from your sister," she said, her voice a shaky whisper. "Your father's missing."

"Missing?" A dozen thoughts and emotions slammed through him. None good. Had their attacker managed to get to his dad?

But Colt didn't even get a chance to ask for more information. That's because the shots started again.

This time all being fired at Buddy.

Buddy leaned out to return fire. Something that Colt couldn't let him do since it could very well be Reed doing the shooting.

Colt took aim at Buddy and would have pulled the trigger.

If someone hadn't beaten him to it.

The bullet slammed into Buddy. His shoulder, from what Colt could tell. That didn't stop Buddy, though.

Still cursing, Buddy came out shooting.

ELISE HAD NO idea what was going on, but with the way Buddy was acting, maybe she'd been wrong about his being behind the attacks. Buddy fired some shots and took off running into the wooded area behind the storage shed.

The moment he disappeared from sight, the shots came at them again.

But that wasn't the only gunfire. She heard someone else shooting. Maybe Reed or Cooper. If so, perhaps they could get this situation under control so they could figure out what'd happened to Colt's father.

Missing, Rosalie had said.

And Elise doubted the man had just taken a late-night stroll. No. He was likely in as much danger as they were.

Maybe more.

She hated to think the worst, but Roy could be dead. Some kind of payback for whatever she'd done to make these monsters launch this attack against her. An attack that had now extended to Colt's family. And to Reed and Darnell.

"Hold your fire!" someone shouted.

Not Buddy this time, but it was a voice that Elise instantly recognized.

Meredith.

That caused the skin to crawl on the back of her neck. There was no good reason for her to be out here at Reed's place. But there was one especially bad reason.

Because maybe she was the one trying to kill them.

Of course, Buddy was out there, so maybe he was the one. Heaven forbid if they'd paired up to launch this attack together.

Despite the injury that Buddy had gotten in the gunfight, it could have all been staged to make everyone think he was innocent. Heck, Buddy could have set all this up as some kind of hoax to rescue them so he could in turn get a lighter sentence for the murder charges that would be filed against him.

"Text Reed again," Colt told her. "See if he knows why Meredith's here."

Elise did, and she got a quick response from Reed. "He doesn't know. Reed didn't even know Meredith was around until she just yelled out."

She'd barely relayed that to Colt when his phone buzzed again. Rosalie. And the message that Elise saw on the screen had her heart jumping to her throat.

Rosalie had found drops of blood on the back porch of the McKinnon home, and there appeared to have been some kind of struggle.

Mercy. What had happened?

"What is it?" Colt asked, glancing over his shoulder at her.

"We need to finish up here so we can find your father," Elise settled for saying. No need to worry Colt further when they were trapped.

But, of course, he was already worried. Colt took the phone from her, read the message for himself and mumbled some profanity. "Tell Cooper he needs to get back to the ranch and find out what's going on."

Elise sent the message, praying that Cooper would get there in time to stop whatever was happening with their father.

"I need help!" Meredith shouted. "Joplin hit me with a Taser, then tied me up and brought me here."

Great. If Joplin was indeed out here, then all their suspects were in one place. Now the problem would be to figure out which one was guilty.

No sign of Joplin, Reed immediately texted. I'm moving closer so cover me.

Elise relayed that to Colt, and he angled his body to give Reed the cover he'd requested. It didn't take long for her to see Reed dart out from some trees behind the woodpile. His gaze fired all around, and he must not have seen anyone, because Reed raced toward them and dropped down on the ground next to them.

"Is Buddy still out there?" Colt asked him.

Reed shook his head. "Didn't see him, but I did spot Meredith. She's on the other side of the house in those trees."

The spot where they'd seen a gunman earlier.

"Anyone with her?" Colt pressed.

"Not that I could tell."

That didn't meant Leo or Joplin wasn't out there hiding.

"What about the dogs?" Elise hoped nothing bad had happened to them.

"Someone Tasered them. They'll be fine, but whoever did it will have to answer to me."

Elise only hoped Reed got the chance to make that happen. Being Tasered was horrible, but at least the person hadn't killed the poor animals.

Reed tipped his head to the shed. "There's still too much smoke in the house. From a smoke bomb, I think.

But we can get Elise in through the back of the shed and wait for Cooper to have more men in place."

"Cooper had to go back to the ranch." Colt paused. "Dad's missing."

"What the hell else could go wrong tonight?" Reed said after he cursed.

Elise was afraid she didn't want to know the answer to that.

"I figure Cooper will send someone else out here," Colt went on. "But in the meantime, let's get Elise out of the line of fire."

No one argued with that. Except her. "I don't want to be tucked away someplace safe while you three are taking all the risks."

Colt shifted his gaze to her, and he looked ready to give her a huge argument about that. Instead, he dropped a kiss on her mouth. Surprising her. Probably surprising Reed and Darnell, too.

"Let's go," Colt told Reed a split second before they started running.

Elise braced herself for more shots to come their way.

But none did.

In fact, the only sounds were their footsteps, ragged breaths and Meredith yelling for someone to untie her. If she was indeed tied up, she was going to have to stay that way for a while. At least until they were certain all the gunmen had been captured or killed.

Once they reached the side of the shed, Colt stopped and peered around the corner. There were two doors, one on the side opposite the woodpile—where Meredith and the other gunmen likely were. The other door was at the rear, and that's obviously the one Colt planned to use. Probably because he thought it would give them the best chance of getting inside before they were gunned down.

It was much darker here than by the house because of the angle of the moon and the trees. Elise considered taking out Colt's phone and using it for illumination, but she didn't want to make themselves a spotlight for the gunman.

"Don't go in yet," Colt warned her when he pulled her behind the shed with him. "Wait here with Reed and Darnell."

Colt went closer, no doubt ready to open the door and check inside to make sure no one was hiding and about to attack. However, he only made it a few steps before he stumbled on something. Elise couldn't see what, but she knew from Colt's profanity that it wasn't good.

"What is it?" she asked, almost afraid to hear the answer.

Colt cursed again and reached down to touch something. "It's a dead body."

Chapter Eighteen

Elise tried to look over Colt's shoulder, but thankfully it was too dark for her to see anything. He hoped. He darn sure didn't want her seeing *this*.

"It's Buddy," he told her.

Her breath stalled in her throat. "He's really dead?"

Colt nodded.

"Oh, God," she whispered.

Colt repeated it under his breath. He'd known that Buddy had been shot, but he hadn't thought it was that serious, especially since Buddy had run from the scene. However, when Reed used his phone for illumination, that's when Colt saw the gunshot wound to the head.

Unfortunately, Elise saw it, too.

"That didn't happen when he was by the woodpile," she said, touching her fingers to her lips.

No, it hadn't. Of course, with all the bullets that'd been flying around, Buddy could have been shot at any time afterward. Still, Colt hadn't heard gunfire coming from this particular direction.

"He was shot at point-blank range," Reed said to him.

Yeah, Colt had noticed that, too. That meant the killer had either sneaked up on Buddy or else Elise's former tenant had trusted the person who'd pulled the trigger.

Colt took hold of her again to lead her away from

Buddy's body and into the shed, but the movement stopped him. It was the sound of footsteps. Not someone trying to sneak up on them, either. These footsteps belonged to someone who was running.

"You've got to help me!" Meredith shouted.

Judging from the sound of her voice, she was headed directly toward them.

"Don't shoot me," Meredith begged. "Please don't shoot."

Despite Colt's moving in front of her, he figured that Elise got a glimpse of the woman making her way across the backyard. She was indeed coming toward the shed.

And Meredith had a gun in her hand.

That got Colt, Reed and Darnell all aiming at her.

But something wasn't right.

Meredith's arms were stiff by her sides, the gun dangling from her hand on the outside of her thigh, and she was staggering, barely able to stay on her feet. Colt, Reed and Darnell obviously realized something was wrong, too, because they didn't fire.

"Joplin wants you to shoot me," she called out to them. "He wants me dead because I know the truth."

"Stop right there," Colt ordered.

Meredith did, but he gave an uneasy glance over his shoulder. "He'll kill me. He'll kill us all."

"You mean Joplin?" Colt challenged.

"Of course," she said, and she came even closer. "He put the duct tape around me and shoved me out from the trees so you'd kill me."

Meredith dropped onto the ground by the side of the shed. That's when Colt could see that there was indeed tape wrapped around her body.

"Why would Joplin want me to kill you?" Colt demanded.

"Because he's crazy, that's why. I overheard him talking on his phone after he left the sheriff's office. He was plotting to kill Elise so she can't testify and clear your father's name. Before I could tell you about what I heard, he had one of his hired thugs Taser me and he brought me here."

That didn't make sense. Unless Joplin had planned on setting up Meredith for all of this. Or maybe Joplin just wanted them to get rid of Meredith since she'd overheard him scheme to commit murder. That was definitely enough motive for Joplin to want Meredith dead—if it'd happened the way she said, that is.

"Help me get out of this tape," Meredith insisted.

No one moved to do that. In fact, Colt stayed in front of Elise, his gun aimed at Meredith while Darnell and Reed kept watch around them.

"Go ahead and check out the shed," Colt said to Reed. "Then get Elise inside it."

Reed opened the door and used his phone to light up the interior. It was a small space crammed with tack and other supplies, so he had to step in, no doubt to make sure no one was lurking in the shadows.

As soon as Reed was inside, the shot rang out.

Heck, not again. Colt was sick and tired of having bullets come their way.

Colt immediately pulled Elise to the ground with him. Darnell dropped down behind them, his gun still ready. Their attention all went to Reed.

Had he been shot?

But he was standing there. Unharmed.

The blast had been so sudden that it took Colt a moment to realize it hadn't come from inside the shed. Instead, it'd come from the direction of the house, and it was soon followed by a second shot.

Then another.

"He's trying to kill me!" Meredith yelled.

And that's exactly what seemed to be happening. Both shots slammed into the shed just above Meredith's head.

Colt still didn't move to help the woman, but he didn't stop Meredith when she scrambled behind the shed with them.

Another shot came their way, this one tearing through the shed. Reed cursed and dropped down.

"Are you hit?" Colt immediately asked him.

Reed shook his head. "I'm fine."

But the words had no sooner left Reed's mouth when there was more movement next to them.

From Meredith.

Before Colt could even turn his attention from Reed and back to Meredith, the woman brought up her gun and put it right to Elise's head.

Colt's stomach went to his knees.

The duct tape had been a ruse. Colt could see that now. The strip only stretched across the front of her body. She'd been free this whole time, and now she was free to try to kill them.

"Drop your gun," Meredith ordered Colt.

Colt shook his head. "You drop yours."

"I should probably clarify something." Meredith's voice was eerily calm. "I'm wired with a communicator, and my brother's on the other end of this line. If you don't drop your gun now, he'll act according to my orders."

"Orders," Colt spat out like profanity. "What orders?"

The corner of Meredith's mouth lifted, and she turned her gun on Colt. "I have your father. If you don't cooperate, he dies."

ELISE GLARED AT the monster holding the gun aimed at Colt.

If Meredith was lying about having Roy, then she was doing a convincing job of it. Of course, anyone who could put together a string of chaos like this was certainly capable of lying through her teeth.

"Why the hell would you take my father?" Colt snapped. He didn't move to put down his gun as Meredith had demanded.

"To make you cooperate, to make this plan work," Meredith readily answered.

Without shifting the gun away from Colt, Meredith motioned toward the back of the house. A moment later, the third gunman stepped out from the shadows and made a beeline toward her.

"If you shoot him, I shoot Colt," Meredith warned Darnell, Reed and her.

Elise's finger tightened on the trigger, but there was no way she could try to end this. Not with Meredith's gun on Colt. Hopefully, Reed and Darnell wouldn't fire, either. They could all get off a shot, but so could Meredith.

A shot that would indeed kill Colt.

The goon with the bulky shoulders came closer, and Elise saw that he had something in his left hand. A phone.

"Show them," Meredith told the man.

He turned the screen in their direction, and Elise had no trouble seeing a photo of Roy, tied up and gagged. He was on the floor, his feet bound as well, and he was glaring right at the person taking the photo.

Colt obviously saw the photo, too, because the muscles in his jaw turned to iron. "Let him go." He didn't shout, but there was definitely a dangerous edge to his tone.

"Not until you cooperate." Meredith glanced at Darnell and Reed. "Sorry that you two got caught up in this, but if you do what I tell you, neither of you will get hurt."

Judging from the sound that Reed made, he didn't believe her. Neither did Elise. Because she knew Meredith's plan included murder.

No way would she leave witnesses behind when she was so desperate to make this asinine plan work.

"Even if we're dead, you might still be brought up on criminal charges because of what's in my report," Elise said. "That is why you're doing this." And it wasn't a question.

"It is, and conversation won't distract me if that's what you're trying to do."

"I'm trying to figure out how you could have gone stark raving mad," Elise snapped.

Meredith didn't even react to that. She turned her attention back to Colt. "I have no intention of me and my brother going to jail for what Elise uncovered, and once you're out of the way, I'll make the report disappear, too."

"But Frank Wellerman's turning it over to the cops," Elise reminded her.

"He can't turn over what he doesn't have. Let's just say my computer skills are good enough to make things like that disappear. And if Wellerman doesn't cooperate, he'll find himself in just as much hot water as you are."

Elise sucked in her breath. "Sweet heaven. Are you going to kill him, too?"

"I'll do whatever it takes," Meredith snapped. "Because this isn't just about me. It's about Leo, too. He's already on probation, and a charge like this could put him away for a long time."

"You mean for life," Colt corrected. "Because the charges aren't just for embezzlement. It's murder. Leo's the one who killed Martinelli, isn't he? Or maybe he just helped you set that explosive. It doesn't matter. Either way, it's still murder."

That tightened Meredith's mouth, but she didn't address Colt, only Elise. "You understand what it's like to protect someone you love. Well, that's what I'm doing. I'm protecting my brother, who I love. I don't want him to spend a minute in jail for offing a lowlife like Martinelli."

Yes, definitely stark raving mad. But that only made Meredith even more dangerous.

"Martinelli tried to kill me when he ran me off the road," Elise said.

"Not kill you. He was supposed to bring you to me so I could get on with my plan to set up Roy. In addition to being a lowlife, Martinelli was an idiot."

Thank goodness. If he'd been more efficient at his job, Elise might already be dead.

"The gun," Meredith reminded Colt, and with a simple motion of her hand, the goon latched on to Colt and dragged him to his feet.

Meredith knocked the gun from Colt's hands while she aimed her own weapon at the rest of them. Since her hired muscle now had his gun trained on Colt, Elise had no choice but to drop her gun.

Reed and Darnell did the same.

Maybe at least one of them had some kind of backup weapon on them, and while Elise was hoping, she added that maybe Meredith wouldn't search for any other weapons before she took them wherever she was planning on taking them.

"How did you even know Colt and Elise were here?" Reed asked.

"I hired someone to watch the sheriff's office, and he used binoculars to look through the window. He saw you give them your keys."

So, Meredith had covered all the bases. Maybe. But Elise was hoping that the woman had missed something. Something that would keep them alive.

"Why not just kill us here?" Elise asked her.

Meredith made a sound to indicate the answer was obvious. "Because I need to be able to pin your death on Roy, and that means having you two at the same place at the same time. Colt and the others will be unfortunate accidents who got in the way when Roy and his hired gun came to kill you so you can't testify against him."

Elise shook her head. "But I did hypnosis and didn't remember anything incriminating against Roy."

"That doesn't matter. All that matters is that Roy will want to stop you from remembering anything that could come up in a future hypnosis session. The McKinnons haven't exactly been quiet about how much they're concerned about what you're going to say when you take the witness stand."

That sent a chill through Elise. She was already shivering from the cold, but that made it worse. "And then you'll kill Roy," she concluded.

"He'll commit suicide," Meredith said as casually as if discussing the weather. "Let's go. Once we have this contained," she added to her hired goon, "then you'll need to do cleanup here."

Elise didn't want to know what that entailed, but she figured Meredith would make sure there was no evidence left behind that could be traced back to her or anyone she'd hired.

"Move," Meredith's man ordered. With Colt in his meaty grip, he started walking, and dragged Colt right along with him.

Elise quickly followed because she wanted to be near Colt in case things turned worse than they already were. Or in case they were able to come up with some way to escape.

But how?

Anything they did right now would endanger Colt.

The hired gun started leading them away from the house, toward the spot where she'd seen the SUV pull off the road earlier.

"Don't count on your brothers or Deputy Pete coming out to help," Meredith told Colt. "They're all out trying to find your dad."

"And I'm sure you planted some false information to send them on a wild-goose chase." Colt mumbled.

Meredith didn't confirm it, but Elise figured that's exactly what the woman had done. However, she couldn't imagine all his family leaving Colt in the middle of a gunfight, so maybe Cooper had arranged for help from one of the deputies of a nearby town.

Elise listened for anyone who might be out there. Obviously, so did Meredith and her hired gun, and they approached the SUV with caution, both of them looking around to make sure they weren't about to be ambushed.

But no one was there.

Well, no one except a driver. Yet another hired thug, no doubt. And that meant Meredith had an extra gun and some muscle to make sure she led them to their deaths.

Colt's gaze met hers, and even though he didn't say a word, she knew he was trying to tell her not to get in the SUV. Once they were inside, Meredith would have even more control over them than she did now.

But what should she do?

She glanced back at Reed and Darnell, who were glancing around as well, no doubt trying to figure out their best way out of this.

Meredith threw open the back door to the SUV. "It'll be a tight squeeze, but I want Colt, Reed and Darnell in the back with Gordy here." She smiled when she looked at Elise. "You'll be up front with me. I think Colt will be less inclined to do something stupid if this gun's pointed at you."

He would be, and that's why they had to do something now.

Meredith took hold of her arm, to shove her onto the seat. But the sound stopped her.

A low, menacing growl.

One of the dogs.

"Get in now!" Meredith yelled, and she volleyed her attention between them and the direction of that growl.

Elise saw the movement from the corner of her eye. Then heard the sound of more movement.

Colt lunged at Meredith, and in the same motion, he pushed Elise out of the way. The hired goon, Gordy, reached for her. No doubt to pull her in front of him and use her as a shield to stop Darnell and Reed.

But it was too late for that.

One of the Dobermans came out of the bushes and went straight for Gordy. The dog knocked the man down, and his gun went flying. Before it even hit the ground, the second dog tore through the bushes to come at the man, too.

That didn't stop the thug behind the wheel, though.

He took aim at Reed and fired.

Reed got out of the way in the nick of time, but he didn't stay down. Darnell and he both went across the seat to grab the guy's gun.

With her heart going way too fast, Elise frantically searched the ground and finally spotted the thug's weapon. She snatched it up and took aim at Meredith. At least she tried, but Colt and the woman were too close. No way could she risk firing a shot because she might hit Colt.

The dogs continued to keep Gordy on the ground, and Reed and Darnell managed to wrestle the gun away from the man behind the wheel.

Then Elise heard another sound.

One that she didn't want to hear.

A shot blasted through the night.

Oh, God.

Meredith still had hold of her gun, and she'd managed to pull the trigger. For one heart-stopping moment, she thought that maybe Colt had been shot. And maybe he had. But she saw him move.

He was alive and still wrestling with Meredith to get that gun away from her.

Nothing could have stopped her at that point. Elise couldn't fire, but she brought back the gun, and with as much strength as she could muster, she bashed it against Meredith's shoulder. Then, the side of her head.

Meredith howled in pain, and even though she didn't move off Colt, it was enough to give Colt the edge. He knocked Meredith's gun from her hand, and in the same motion, he pinned Meredith to the ground. Colt didn't waste a second. He got to his feet and dragged Meredith to hers.

Thank God, it was over.

Elise handed Colt the gun, and Reed and Darnell

came out of the SUV. Reed had a firm grip on the hired gun. With just a low whistle, the dogs stopped their attack and backed away. However, Elise was pretty sure Gordy was too injured to do much fighting back.

Reed took some plastic cuffs from his pocket to restrain the guy, and he handed a pair to Colt to use on Meredith. "Let's get this trash to jail," Reed grumbled.

But Meredith laughed. "You think you've won but you haven't."

"What the hell does that mean?" Colt snarled, and he pushed Meredith into the backseat of the SUV.

"It means I have someone holding your father. Or did you forget?"

"I didn't forget," Colt assured her and caught onto the collar of her coat. "Where is he?"

Meredith laughed again. "If I can't get back at Elise, at least I have the pleasure of knowing that your father's dead. Or at least he will be soon if I don't make a call to save him."

"Where is he?" Colt repeated.

"There's only one way you can save him." Meredith paused, her oily smile aimed at Colt. "Let me go now, and your father gets to live. Once I'm out of the country, I'll call and tell you where to find him."

"Right." Colt added some profanity. "Like I'd trust you after everything you've done."

"You don't have a choice," Meredith insisted, staring him right in the eyes.

"I think I do." Colt caught onto Meredith and tossed her out of the SUV and onto the ground. "Watch them, and call my brothers," Colt told Reed. "I'm going after my dad."

Chapter Nineteen

Colt didn't want to risk taking his truck in case Meredith or one of her henchmen had managed to plant some explosives in it. So he jumped behind the wheel of the SUV. The problem was that Elise got in with him, as well.

"I'm going with you," she insisted, and he could tell from her tone and body language that it wouldn't do any good to argue with her.

And he wouldn't.

For one thing, he needed to get to his father ASAP and didn't want to waste even a second. For another, he wasn't sure that he wanted Elise at Reed's place, what with the dead bodies and the chaos. At least if she was with him, Colt could make sure she was all right. Of course, so far his track record at keeping her safe wasn't that good.

Something he'd kick himself for later.

Elise buckled up and looked at him. "I think your father's at my house. I think the photo was taken in my living room."

"Yeah." Colt had already come to that conclusion, too, and that's the direction he headed. "I figure Meredith would want to do the murders there. Maybe to make it look as if my father broke in to kill you so he could silence you."

Of course, that didn't explain what Meredith had planned to do with his, Darnell's and Reed's bodies. Maybe she'd planned on setting up his father for that, as well. Maybe Meredith could have made it look as if Roy had gone insane.

When it was Meredith who'd gone off the deep end.

The woman would pay for what she'd done, but Colt prayed his dad didn't become another casualty.

"Are you okay?" Colt asked her. He was almost afraid to take a closer look. With everything that'd gone on tonight, it was possible she had injuries he didn't even know about.

"I wasn't hurt," she said, her voice almost soundless. She cleared her throat, repeated it. "How about you?"

"We're both alive," he settled for saying. Though he figured the nightmares would be with him for a long time.

Other memories, too.

Ones that he didn't want to deal with right now, not until he was sure his father was safe.

His phone buzzed, and that's when he remembered that Elise still had it. She fished it from her pocket, and when she saw Cooper's name on the screen, she put the call on speaker.

"I just talked to Reed," Cooper greeted. "What the hell's going on?"

"Long story," Colt answered. "But Elise and I are on our way to her place now. We think that's where Meredith has someone holding Dad, and we're about ten minutes out."

Cooper cursed. "I'm not that far from there—less

than five minutes. Pete and one of the ranch hands are with me."

Colt wanted any and all help right now. "Elise is with me, and we're in a black SUV that Meredith brought to Reed's place. So, don't shoot when you see the strange vehicle."

"Thanks for the heads-up. The only reason we're out here is because we got a message saying Dad was being held at the old Saunders farm."

Colt had been right about Meredith's attempts to throw them off track. And, heck, maybe he was still wrong about the location, but he prayed he wasn't.

If he was wrong about this, it could cost his dad his life.

"Is everyone else okay at the ranch?" Colt asked. "Did Meredith hurt anyone?"

"Everyone's fine. What I want to know—was Meredith working alone?"

"Her brother's probably involved, and she hired some muscle. Two of them are dead at Reed's place, but I'm pretty sure she wasn't working with Buddy. He's dead, too," Colt added.

That caused Cooper to curse some more, and Colt heard the soft shudder that left Elise's mouth. He slid his hand over hers and wished he could do more to soothe those frayed nerves. Of course, it was going to take a lot more than hand-holding and hugging to do that.

"Well, Meredith wasn't working with Joplin," Cooper continued. "Joplin's at the sheriff's office right now. Apparently, Meredith tried to kidnap him first so she could set him up, but Joplin got away. That's when she went after Dad."

"Is Joplin okay?" Colt asked.

"He's shaken up, but he'll be fine. He's already talking about getting ready for the trial."

"Good," Elise and Colt said in unison. Despite how they felt about Joplin and Jewell's upcoming trial, they already had enough injured people and dead bodies without adding more.

"I shouldn't have slept with you," Colt mumbled.

Oh, man.

He definitely hadn't intended to say that aloud. Especially not with his brother still listening.

"Uh, I guess this is a good time for me to hang up," Cooper said. "I'll be at Elise's place in a couple of minutes. I'll see you there."

"Yeah," Colt assured him, and he hung up, glancing at Elise to give her a real apology instead of that ill-timed mumble.

"Don't you dare," she warned him before he could say a word. She sounded a whole lot stronger than she had just several moments earlier. "You can regret sleeping with me if you want, but for the record, I don't regret it one bit."

"Well, you should. If I hadn't been on that floor with you, I might have seen the gunman coming sooner."

"Really? Even though the dogs hadn't seen him yet?" She didn't wait for an answer. "Sex didn't cause the attack, and it didn't obligate you to anything, so I darn sure don't want an apology."

All right. She was clearly mad at him or something he'd said, but Colt wasn't sure why. Added to that, he really didn't have the time to figure it out. They were just a couple of miles from her place, and he needed to establish some ground rules before they arrived.

"We'll table the apology for now," he said. "But when we get to your house, I don't want you out of my sight until I know it's safe. You've already dodged enough bullets tonight."

"So have you." That was the same argumentative tone. And she gave a heavy sigh afterward. "Whatever you do, just stay safe."

Oh, he would, and he'd keep her safe, too. Even if Meredith had planned some surprises for them.

Turning off his headlights, Colt made the turn to her ranch and then slowed so he could check out their surroundings. He immediately spotted Cooper's truck.

Headlights off, too.

And it was parked a good twenty yards from the house, the truck hidden in some trees. He didn't see his brother right away and the men he'd brought with him, but Colt figured they were making their way to the house where they would find his father alive and well.

He refused to believe differently.

Colt pulled to a stop near his brother's truck and reached to open the door. But then he stopped. With the sick plans that Meredith had put in place, it was best not to risk leaving her alone in case Meredith had another goon standing by, ready to grab her.

The woman sure had done some stupid things to protect herself. And her brother. Meredith had also done those stupid things in the name of love.

Yeah, love could do that to a person sometimes.

Even though he'd meant that thought for Meredith, Colt couldn't help but realize that he wasn't immune to that, either. Maybe not love exactly...

Or maybe that was exactly what it was.

"What's wrong now?" Elise asked.

"Nothing." He got his thoughts back on track and tipped his head to the house. "Stay behind me when we get out, and once we're closer, I'll have Pete and the ranch hand stay with you."

She nodded, looking a little uncertain. Maybe because she didn't want to jump back in the path of danger. Or maybe it was because of his *nothing* answer. Once his father was safe, he needed to clear his head and figure out how to finish this conversation.

They got out, Elise following behind him as he'd ordered, and they made their way to Cooper's truck. His brother and the others weren't there, but he quickly located them thanks to the milky-white light spearing from the front window and into the darkness.

Pete was on the left side of the house. The ranch hand, Zeke Mercer, on the right. And Cooper was on the porch standing next to the door and peering into the window.

Cooper must have seen something inside because he motioned for Colt and the others to stay quiet. Colt did, and he hurried Elise to the house and put her on the side next to Pete so he could join his brother. One look in the window and Colt's heart went to his knees.

His father was on the floor, not moving.

Colt had to fight through the punch of fear and dread, but he finally saw why his dad wasn't moving. His hands and feet were tied. Trussed up like an animal with his mouth taped shut, and Leo was seated at Elise's table while he chowed down on a bag of fast food. Meredith's brother didn't appear to have any backup with him.

Probably because he'd trusted that his sister's plan would work.

Big mistake.

Colt kicked in the door and rushed inside, with Cooper right behind him. Leo reached for his gun.

"Go head," Colt warned him. "See how fast you die."

And he meant it. He was sick and tired of all these idiots Meredith had used to try to destroy their lives.

Leo thought about it. Colt could see the debate on his face, but he also glanced at the two guns pointed right at him. Cursing, Leo stood and lifted his hands in surrender.

Colt made a quick check of his father. He didn't appear to be harmed, so while Cooper dealt with Leo, Colt checked out the rest of the house. Room by room.

It was empty, thank God.

By the time Colt made it back into the living room, Cooper had handcuffed Leo, and Pete and Elise had rushed in to help untie his father.

Later, Colt would fuss at her for not staying back until he'd made sure the house was clear. But for now, he was just thankful to have Elise, his family and the others alive and safe.

He hugged his father. Cooper joined in. And his father surprised him a little by hooking his arm around Elise and drawing her into the family embrace.

"You got Meredith?" his father asked.

Colt nodded. "We got her."

Roy looked at Elise, pushing her hair from her face so he could examine the stitches on her forehead. A fresh bruise was just below it, and the sight of it turned Colt's stomach.

He'd come way too close to losing her tonight.

It was that reminder that had Colt pulling her into his arms when his father and Cooper stepped away. His brother didn't miss the close contact between Elise and him, and Colt only deepened the contact when he brushed a kiss on her cheek.

Cooper handed off the prisoner to Pete, and his

brother's eyebrow lifted. "That's the best you can do?" Cooper asked him.

Colt was sure he scowled. This was about that slip of the tongue he'd made to Elise while still on the phone with Cooper.

I shouldn't have slept with you.

Heck, how many times would Cooper use that to taunt him? Judging from the glimmer in his eye, often.

"Pete and I need to take this guy to jail," Cooper added, a hint of a smile bending his mouth. "Zeke can take Dad to the hospital—"

"Not a chance," Roy interrupted. "I'm fine, but Elise might need to go."

She shook her head. "I'm okay, really."

But she wasn't okay. Far from it. She was shaking so hard Colt pulled her deeper into his arms. That's when he realized she didn't even have a coat, so he pulled a throw blanket from the back of the sofa and wrapped it around her. He got her moving outside and toward the SUV so he could take her and his dad out of there.

"Talk to her," Cooper whispered to Colt as they headed down the steps. "Grovel if necessary. Just don't be an idiot and let her get away again."

Because it was a habit for him to disagree with his big brother, Colt opened his mouth to do that. Then he realized what a stupid mistake that would be.

"I was wrong," Colt said to Elise. She was in midstep but stopped and stared at him.

"Yes, you were. It wasn't a mistake to sleep with me."

Thankfully, his father and Zeke were wise enough to keep on walking toward the SUV so they'd have some privacy. Even Cooper cooperated. While on each side of their prisoner, they headed toward Cooper's truck.

Giving Colt some much-needed time to trip over whatever the heck he was about to say to make this right.

But Elise spoke before he could.

"I'm in love with you," she blurted out. "Now, I know that doesn't make things easier. Not for you, not for me. I still want to make a go of this place and turn it back into a working ranch. That means I'm not going anywhere, and you'll have to learn to live with it."

"You're right," Colt said, giving that some thought. "It doesn't make it easier. But it does make it better."

She blinked, but before she could say anything else, Colt decided to do what he did best. And it wasn't talking.

He hauled Elise to him and kissed her.

Colt didn't make it a quick peck, either. He kissed her long, hard and deep. Until she made a throaty sigh and melted against him. Then he kissed her again.

"That's better," she repeated.

"Yeah, I thought so." And despite the bad night, he found himself smiling.

Well, he smiled until Elise shook her head. She was no doubt about to launch into lots of things that were all minor now that he knew how things were between them.

And things between them were definitely *better*.

Colt wanted a whole lot more than that, though.

"You will make a go of this ranch," he assured her. "And I'll help you. It's a good thing you're not going anywhere because I'm head over heels in love with you."

Elise froze, pulling in her breath, before a slow smile formed on her mouth. "You actually said it. I didn't think you would."

"Well, obviously I'll have to say it a lot more often." And he did. "I love you, Elise. I really love you."

That earned him another smile. Another kiss, too,

and Elise was just as good at it as he was. They made a great team.

"You'll marry me?" he asked.

"Of course." She nipped his bottom lip with her teeth. "You'll share your bed with me tonight?"

Colt couldn't think of a better way to seal the deal. He scooped up Elise in his arms and kissed her.

* * * * *

USA TODAY *bestselling author Delores Fossen's*
SWEETWATER RANCH *miniseries continues*
next month with REINING IN JUSTICE.
Look for it wherever
Harlequin Intrigue books are sold!